Hidden Treasure

Book Two in The Lost Andersons

By

Melody Anne

HIDDEN TREASURE

Book Two of The Lost Andersons

ISBN-13: 978-1499193664
ISBN-10: 1499193661

Cover Art by Edward
Edited by Alison
Interior Design by Adam

www.melodyanne.com

Email: info@melodyanne.com

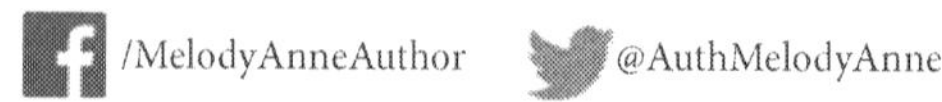 /MelodyAnneAuthor  @AuthMelodyAnne

First Edition
Printed in the U.SA

DEDICATION

This is dedicated to my longtime friend Adam, someone I trust more than any other. I couldn't do this without your taking care of everything in my life. I'm so thankful to know you, love you, and have you always be there for me and my family!

NOTE FROM THE AUTHOR

I'm so excited about this story because you get to meet some of the characters for my upcoming book series with Simon & Schuster's Pocket Books. Those books are set in Montana, which just so happens to be where Brielle gets her ranch. I love intertwining my characters from the different series so that we can all keep up with them, because when I write these stories these characters become a part of my family and I just don't want to let them go.

There's no possible way I could do what I love so much without an entire team of people behind me. I want to thank them so much.

* Jack Martin, who does so many things above and beyond the call of duty

* My manager, Adam, who never fails to take care of it all.

* Kathiey, who runs the social media side of things, but that's just the tip of the iceberg — she's amazing

* My editors — Alison, Nikki, and Mary — who argue with me, encourage me, and make me a better writer

* Jeff, who is the numbers guy (and daddy to my amazing nephews and future niece) and makes sure we are all taken care of.

* Eddie, who probably believes he's fallen into the Twilight Zone working with me

* Aunt Linda, who makes sure my home stays perfect

* My two best friends, Nik and Stephy, who always share ideas, inspiration, and dirty thoughts

* My husband, who takes care of me so much more than most husbands would ever dream of doing. He goes above and beyond every single day.

* My beautiful daughter, Phoenix, who storyboards with me, and inspires me to be a better person

* Chris, who has helped me with this book and done storyboarding with me, much to his horror, and given me flight and ranch information

* My nephews, Jacob and Isaiah, and Kathiey's grandkids, Ryder, Maycie, Reese and Kaylee, who take my stress away by spending the day with them

* My mother, who gave me a love of romance

There are so many more people in my life that inspire and help me that I could write a book just about them alone. I love you all.

Finally, a huge thanks to my Muses, my beta readers, and my fans. Because of you, I get to live my dreams.

Melody Anne

OTHER BOOKS BY MELODY ANNE

Billionaire Bachelors:
*The Billionaire Wins the Game
*The Billionaire's Dance
*The Billionaire Falls
*The Billionaire's Marriage Proposal
*Blackmailing the Billionaire
*Run Away Heiress
*The Billionaire's Final Stand

The Lost Andersons:
*Unexpected Treasure
*Hidden Treasure
*Holiday Treasure
*Priceless Treasure

Baby for the Billionaire:
*The Tycoon's Revenge
*The Tycoon's Vacation
*The Tycoon's Proposal
*The Tycoon's Secret
*The Lost Tycoon

Surrender:
*Surrender - Book One
*Submit - Book Two
*Seduced - Book Three
*Scorched - Book Four

Forbidden Series:
*Bound -Book One
*Broken - Book Two
*Betrayed - Book Three
*Burned - Book Four

OTHER BOOKS BY MELODY ANNE (CONT.)

Unexpected Heroes:
*Her Unexpected Hero
*Who I am With You - Novella
*Her Hometown Hero
*Following Her - Novella
*Her Forever Hero - (February 2016)

*Safe in His Arms - Novella - Baby, It's Cold Outside Anthology

Rise of the Dark Angel:
*Midnight Fire
*Midnight Moon
*Midnight Storm
*Midnight Eclipse (December 8th, 2015)

PROLOGUE

SHE REFUSED TO cry. She hadn't done that in eleven years.

So Brielle Storm inspected her fingernails, tapped her foot, and waited for the show to begin with all the coolness she could muster. It had been a couple of days since her last manicure. Yes, that's what she would focus on. It was easier to focus on her nails, and to keep her family thinking she was nothing more than a shallow, spoiled brat, than to have them know what she really was.

But did she even know herself? No. Not really. She'd been lost for so many years, she didn't think it possible to find herself. Finding yourself was a sixties thing, anyway. So she would focus on her fingers, look at the chipped paint on her nails, and tune out the people who used to be the most important ones in her life.

A spa was calling her name, wasn't it? Of course it was.

As the sound of serial muttering floated around her, she looked up, annoyed that she had to deal with her family. Why on earth had her father summoned them? They'd been little more than strangers to each other for a long time. And Brielle liked it that way. Well… That was her story, and she was sticking to it. There was no room for emotion in the world she'd come to be a part of. These people in the room with her were little more than strangers now. Tuning back into the conversation, she made her face into a mask of boredom as one of her brothers spoke.

"Do any of you have a clue what this is about?"

"Nope. It seems the old man has gotten something up his keister again," another brother said. "I still haven't gone to bed yet — sheesh, I'd been up all night when my phone rang with dad's summons. I seriously considered not showing up."

Brielle smiled, the forced social smile she knew her brothers detested. "You might as well stop complaining about it, because you know how father gets. You don't want your precious trust fund cut off, now, do you?"

"Shut up, Brielle. You're the one who'd be hurting if you lost Daddy's money."

The comment stung, but she refused to acknowledge it. She wouldn't show weakness in front of her brothers — no way. There was a time she'd thought of them all as superheroes, thought the sun and moon hung on them.

That time was long over.

So why was she suddenly fighting tears?

Nope. Wasn't going to happen, because Brielle didn't cry — not anymore.

She deleted that emotion and looked toward her oldest brother, Crew, with a subdued scowl. Then Lance spoke and she turned in his direction. Lance was the second of the boys their turncoat mother had popped out of her belly at regular intervals before she took off in the middle of the night.

"All of you should shut up before the old man walks in. The more compliant we are, the sooner this touching family reunion can end, and the quicker we can get on with our lives."

"That's very good thinking, Lance. I know how important it is for you to run from my presence."

Her father's voice.

Brielle tensed as the man of the hour came through the doorway. He had once been the biggest hero of all to her. Now she barely spoke to him. As she sat motionless, she waited, wishing for only a brief second that she could turn back the clock, and be that little girl again who ran into her father's arms without the weight of sorrow on her back that kept her from doing so now. But she quickly pushed that thought away. No emotions! That was her motto.

"Fine, you heard us complaining," Brielle said. "We're sorry, Dad, but we haven't all been together in one room in years. So what's the big emergency?" Even though it was morning, she stood and walked to the liquor cabinet and poured herself a scotch. It was just a dramatic gesture, really, all for show. She didn't make a habit of drinking, especially at eight a.m.

If truth were to be told, she hated the whiskey, hated her life, hated the empty shell she felt she had become.

But she wouldn't tell her father that. And she certainly wouldn't share with her brothers. She was the baby of the family at age twenty-four, but she wasn't about to act like one. She didn't respect them — even her father. And she didn't particularly respect herself. What was the point of even being there with them now? Tipping her glass back, she swallowed, enjoying the burn as the scotch slid down her throat. At least that was something else to focus on instead of these thoughts running through her head, instead of the pain of being in the room with a family she no longer felt was family.

"You've all been cut out of my will and I'm freezing your trust funds."

It took Brielle a few moments to process her father's words, but when she did, she found herself white-knuckling her empty glass. Had she heard correctly?

"Do you care to elaborate?" Crew asked, his face devoid of emotion.

It ran in the family, Brielle thought.

"My parents were hard workers their entire lives. They built not only one medical practice, but two. They scrimped and saved, and gave me a good education. When they passed, I was devastated, but I took my inheritance and I created something both of them would be proud of. Unfortunately, I've pampered and indulged the five of you, making you think that life is nothing more than one big party, and that you deserve to be handed everything on a silver platter. Well, that stops today. As I've just said, you've been cut from my will. Your trust funds are frozen, and your credit cards canceled —"

"You can't do that!" Ashton shouted.

Amen, Brielle said silently.

"I can and I have. You may leave the room now and be on your way, or you can hear me out." None of them budged as their father turned to each of them looked them in the eye. Much to her horror, Brielle again felt tears threaten.

No!

That was a weakness she wouldn't show, especially in this room. Never again. She hadn't shed one tear since she was thirteen years old. Not one!

"You haven't really given us a choice other than to listen to you, have you?" Lance said. "Is this your way of saying you need some attention? You could have just scheduled a lunch date." He was trying to make a joke, but the mood in the room allowed no break in the tension.

"You always have a choice, Lance. It's your decision whether to make the right one or not. I'm really sorry you feel that way, though. It honestly breaks my heart. We were once a tight-knit family, laughing together, speaking often, *living* our lives. I don't know where I went wrong, but somewhere along the way, you got lost, and now I'm allowing you to find yourselves again. I hope you do."

Brielle rolled her eyes. "Okay, okay. What is this 'journey' you want us to take?" Good. She'd regained her composure and she could think more clearly. Best to just get this meeting over with.

"I'm glad you asked, Peaches," he replied, reverting to the nickname he'd given her at birth. The sun-kissed color of her hair was as stunning as the beginning rays of a sunset, and it hadn't changed as she grew older.

She hadn't been called that in ages, and for one brief moment, she was knocked out of kilter. It was a name of love, of better times. And those days were over.

Brielle pulled herself together and looked back at her father with now-narrowed eyes. "I haven't been *Peaches* in fifteen years, *Daddy*, but if you want to reminisce about the 'good' old days, then I'll go ahead and play your game."

The tone of her voice seemed to make her father stumble slightly, and Brielle couldn't help but feel immense guilt. But she *couldn't* feel that — *wouldn't* feel it. She didn't love her father anymore. He was just a weak old man, she told herself. He'd been as self-absorbed as the rest of them. Or just work-absorbed.

"I've sold the family business. I've decided it's time for a fresh start, and I've chosen to do it on the West Coast. There's nothing in Maine to hold me here any longer, and I'm tired of the tourist season. I've just finalized the paperwork on a failing computer tech firm, and I plan to turn it around. Doing that gave me an idea for the five of you."

Rage simmered in Lance's eyes. "Can this be reversed?" His voice was strained with the amount of control he had to exert to keep his temper.

"No." Richard didn't elaborate.

"The business was supposed to be mine."

"Then you should have taken pride in it. You should have proved to me that you deserved a stake in the family business. I had hoped to pass it to you one day, but as of right now, you are unworthy to take the reins of any business of mine."

Crew broke in. "Don't you think that's a bit harsh, Father?"

"No, I don't, Crew. And you are no different from your brother Lance. None of you has worked for an honest dollar in so long, I can't remember when last you did, and I would rather see my funds passed down to people who can appreciate them than leave them to you with the way you've been acting. You have time to figure this out — well, time for now, at least."

"What is *that* supposed to mean — *for now*?" Tanner asked.

"Nothing, Tanner. You just need to pay attention. I want you to prove yourselves, make something of your lives. You are more than these spoiled brats I see before me right now."

"How are we supposed to do anything if we have no money? What do you want us to do to *prove* ourselves?" Tanner threw his hands into the air in exasperation.

"That's the smartest question you've asked so far," Richard said with a smile before pausing to gaze at each one of his children. "I've purchased five more failing businesses. You can fight amongst yourselves to choose which one you want to run. I've created a sufficient budget for you to do what needs to be done to bring the companies back into profitability. If you do this, and do it well, only then will I reinstate your inheritance. If you fail, you will be on your own."

"Well, what if your idea of a successful business is different from what our idea would be?" Ashton asked.

"When you truly feel success for the first time in your life, you will know what it is. You've never earned that badge of honor before. You'll learn now, one way or the other. I'm done explaining this. You may come see me when you're ready."

Setting down the manila folders of the five businesses he'd bought, he looked each of his children in the eye again, then turned to leave the room.

Brielle was fuming, and she refused even to glance over at the folders. What in the hell was her father thinking? She didn't know how to run a business, let alone make a failing one successful.

This was nothing more than a waste of her time. She flung herself into a deep-cushioned chair. She just wasn't going to play. But as her brothers walked to the table and began grabbing the folders, she felt her fingers twitching. Did she have any other choice?

Yes, she did. No freaking folder for her.

"I'm out of here," she said as she stood back up on wobbly legs and began walking to the door.

"Are you sure you want to do that, Brielle?" Lance asked. "Your manicures don't come cheap."

Brielle turned on her four-inch heels with fire in her eyes. She was in no way beaten, and she wouldn't let Lance push her around. She approached her brother with grave determination. When she was standing only inches from his face, she lifted her hand and poked a sharp fingernail against his chest.

"Don't worry about me, big brother. I have my own ideas."

Lance didn't bother replying, and Brielle was battling strong emotions. Not good. Feigning indifference, she sauntered to the door and pushed her way through it.

This wasn't over, not by a long shot.

CHAPTER ONE

One year later

BRIELLE TOOK DEEP breaths and watched the floor numbers click higher and higher. Why was she in Seattle? And why was she here to beg? Because she'd run out of options.

She'd really thought she would be fine on her own. She'd worked in a retail shop in a mall in Washington D.C., thrilled to leave Maine behind, even though it had meant also leaving her beloved condo and moving into a tiny studio apartment. But the place she'd been working had gone out of business, and she couldn't get another job to save her life. She'd sold off most of what she owned to make the move, but the whole "adventure" had bought her only a little time — a year, to be exact.

So here she was, in her father's new office building. No, she wasn't the master of her fate, but she was still unbowed. More precisely, she was more than ticked off. If Richard thought he'd earn back his place in her heart by forcing her hand, he was dead wrong. What he had done was manipulative and degrading. Yes, she was ticked, but beyond that she was showing the first inklings of real fear.

Upon reaching the top floor, she stopped breathing as the doors opened onto a beautiful lobby. It was smaller than her dad's executive office space on the East Coast, but it was just as classy, and the same secretary he'd had for the past twenty years was sitting behind a huge mahogany desk.

"Good morning, Brielle. It's been a long time," Tanya said with a genuine smile.

Brielle had always liked Tanya, but she couldn't let down her defenses, not right now, so her reply was less than warm: "I'm here to see my father." Instant remorse filled her when the woman, who'd always been kind to her, flinched. "I'm sorry, Tanya," Brielle told her. "I..." Her words had to trail off — she didn't know what to say.

"It's okay, darling. I understand," Tanya said, but it was obvious that she didn't.

Brielle sighed. "No. It's not." She gave the woman a rueful smile, then turned and moved toward her father's office. Being cold was how she survived. It was awful, and she knew it, but it was the only way she made it through each day. Trying to erase the awkwardness with Tanya from her mind, she came to the end of the hallway, where she found an open door.

Of course his office was facing the water. Her father had always loved the ocean, even after losing his parents in a boating accident.

Enough of this. Brielle refused to get sentimental. She was here on business, and she had no time for anything else. She was here to get her father to bend to her will. Or maybe to her wiles.

Turning her lips up in a determined smile, she walked through her father's door. Richard looked up and a grin spread across his face. It was nearly blinding and caused Brielle to stop in her tracks. When was the last time she'd entered a room and found someone so happy to see her? She honestly couldn't remember.

Her protective wall seemed to crack just a little. Heck, she really wanted to rush forward and cling to her father the way she used to do when she was younger and found herself frightened or hurt.

But times had changed. She needed to remember that. She wasn't a little girl anymore and she didn't need anyone, especially not her father. Repairing the wall around her heart, she started moving again — was her stride suitably confident? — and then sat down across from Richard without a word.

"It's so good to see you, Brielle. I'm glad you made your way to Seattle," Richard said, his smile not deflating in the least despite the cool look she was sending his way.

"You really left me with no choice, Father," she replied, trying to tone down the bitterness in her voice but not quite managing to pull it off.

She'd had to take a bus to Seattle. A bus! The trip had taken three days. Three days of pure hell.

"Again, I will say that I'm very sorry I had to do things the way I did, but I need for you all to understand that anything in this life worth having is worth working for."

"This whole rescuing-a-failing-business thing is stupid, Father. I don't know anything about business. Do you remember my college major? You're setting me up for failure, and you know it."

"I would never do that. I love you, Brielle. I know how strong and capable you are. Heck, from the moment you were born, you had your brothers and me wrapped around your tiny little fingers," he said with a chuckle.

"The only business that's left is a stupid ranch in *Montana*."

"I know. Your brothers have already taken possession of the other businesses. I'm very pleased to be seeing results already."

"I can't go to Montana!"

"I hope that's not true, Peaches, because I think it's just the place you need to be."

"I'm not *Peaches* anymore!" She obviously couldn't pull this off. She was too dang upset.

"You will always be my baby girl. I love your brothers dearly, but you will always hold more of my heart than anyone else. And I know you can do this. I wouldn't have asked you to do a task I thought you'd fail at."

They gazed at each other for several moments. Two personalities so much alike in some ways, but so different in others. But the bottom line was that Brielle knew he had the upper hand, knew he didn't need to back down. He knew that, too.

"And if I do fail, I lose everything?"

"Failure isn't an option. You're a Storm."

"You don't know me anymore, Father!"

"I know you better than you think, Brielle. You're a fighter. I got lazy as a parent and forgot how to raise you, but it's never too late. Don't give up before you've had even a chance to see yourself shine."

"Crew gets to be in sunny California and I have to go to Montana. How is that fair?"

"You shouldn't have taken so long to choose."

"So I'm being punished because I didn't want to play your game?"

"You're not being punished at all, Brielle. I know you'll figure that out once you've decided to put your heart and soul into this."

"Well, it sure as hell feels like a punishment."

"I understand that, darling, but go to Montana and I promise that you'll find yourself."

He had to be crazy. How could she find herself amongst a bunch of cows?

"I need money. I have nothing," she told him. If she could just get enough to get by for a little while, she'd manage to find another job, and she'd show him that she didn't need him to prove herself a success.

"You have a budget to work with," he said, then paused before speaking again. "You'll get it once you reach Montana."

"And how am I supposed to get there? It took the last of my funds for the damn bus ticket here." She was still ticked he hadn't even paid for an economy-class flight.

"I will get you there."

Brielle greeted his words with silence, but she knew she'd been defeated.

She'd go, but only because she had no other options before her. She wouldn't succeed, and she knew it. Still, it would be a place to rest her head, a place where she could figure things out and begin mapping out her next steps.

Yes, she would go. But she certainly didn't have to be happy about it.

CHAPTER TWO

IT WAS A freaking nightmare. Sure, most ranches probably had dusty old trucks, and what else did she expect to be waiting for her at the ridiculously small airport in Sterling? But the rusty orange clunker didn't even have air conditioning!

And now that she'd managed to get this antique off and running — sort of — she was hit with another shock as she looked at the house standing before her. What could she say about it? Country bumpkin?

She stood aghast in her stiletto heels and stared at the giant monstrosity of an ugly house before her. It was large, that was for sure, with a huge wraparound covered porch that some people might have found appealing, but Brielle wasn't the type of girl to hang around on a front porch. Screw that quaint little rocking loveseat; she'd never use it in a zillion years.

The house was in desperate need of a paint job, and the windows looked as if they hadn't been updated — ever. Taking a cautious step forward in the dirt and gravel, she let out a very unladylike curse as she stubbed her toe and broke a manicured nail, her high-heeled sandals offering zero protection.

"This can't work. There's no possible way," she muttered. How could her father do this to her?

She could come up with only one answer: *Because he doesn't love me.*

Think about it. There was just no way that the man who had raised her could love her. He'd put her in the wilds of Montana with a bunch of cows and wheat fields. Ten thousand acres of that stupid wheat and those wretched cows. Or bulls. Or whatever.

The only thing she knew about cows was that they tasted damn good when prepared by a top-level chef. Maybe that wasn't sensitive — some of her best friends were vegetarians. But get real. She knew nothing about the world's bovine population, and she wanted to keep it that way. Sensitivity had its limits.

Once she finally made it to the wide front steps, Brielle reached a tentative hand out to the railing. It didn't look sturdy enough to hold her weight, and she didn't weigh much. She made sure of that.

When the rail didn't rock, she felt better, but not much. Holding on tight, she made her way up. But when she reached the porch, she felt a tickle on her hand. *Crap!* She looked down to see a huge, hairy, ugly-ass spider scurrying across her fingers. And Brielle lost it.

Screaming as if she were being attacked, she jerked her hand back, lost her balance and went tumbling backward, landing hard on the dry grass, dirt and rocks in front of the steps. She felt a bruise forming on her rump, and then Brielle did something she hadn't done since she was thirteen years old. Twelve years of repressed emotions ended in one hell of a tantrum.

"I hate it here!" she shrieked, feeling like a fool but not caring. She hadn't been at the ranch for five minutes and already her world was crumbling. "Spiders, cobwebs, rocks, dirt, grime, and who knows what else! Lions and tigers and bears..."

Her angry tears soon stopped, but Brielle was still in a foul mood as she sat there trying to breathe normally. After a few moments, she pulled herself together. Wasn't she better than this? When she heard the crunch of footsteps behind her, she grimaced, not wanting to deal with anyone or anything else right then.

Whipping her head around, she got ready to tell whoever it was to go away when her tongue got stuck on the roof of her mouth. When the person who'd invaded her privacy spoke, she felt even more disoriented.

"May I help you?"

Brielle couldn't seem to find her voice. Since she was still sitting on the ground, the man standing before her was so tall, he seemed to block out the sun. His boots looked old, his jeans dusty — like that truck — and the shirt plastered to his chest had seen better days. Brielle tilted her neck all the way back to examine his face, which was shadowed by the brim of his faded cowboy hat.

"Are you real?" she asked.

When his lips tilted up in a sardonic smile, she thought for a moment that she might be fantasizing. No, not likely. Where she was from, girls never fantasized about cowboys — she preferred a man in a suit. Still, she had to admit, if only to herself, that the guy towering over her was one hell of a hot piece of man candy.

And then he spoke again. "You must be Brielle Storm. I'm Colt Westbrook."

The velvet-voiced giant of a man held out a hand to help her up, and his deep drawl sent an unwelcome shiver down her spine. And yet Brielle found herself hesitating to give him her hand.

Nonsense! She wasn't attracted to him, and she did need to stand up eventually.

Firming her shoulders — it helped that they were on the ground — she stuck out her hand. When his fingers clasped hers and he lifted her up easily, Brielle felt her breath rush from her lungs. But when he held her hand just a moment too long to be appropriate, Brielle finally tugged against him, needing to step back.

"Thank you, Colt. Do you work for me? You must if you know my name." Thank heaven her voice had come out smooth and controlled, that it was finally working again!

His eyes crinkled as if something she'd said had amused him. She was more puzzled now, but quickly covered that up with a snotty comment — her specialty. "I asked a question. Would it be too much to expect an answer?"

He chuckled. But all he said was "No, ma'am."

What in the hell did that mean? No, he didn't work for her, or no, she shouldn't expect an answer? Was this place already messing with her head? Was she living in some alternate reality where she found herself instantly attracted to the wrong sort of man, and she couldn't understand the language?

Baloney. This was nothing but nonsense. Firming her shoulders again, she decided to bail out. "All right, Colt. I'm tired, not happy about being here, and so not into playing games." If he wouldn't answer her simple question, she would just walk away.

Besides, his smell was now beginning to drift over her, and the combination of sweat, leather, and something else she couldn't pin down was making a few butterflies flutter low in her belly, which again made zero sense. She loved cologne, expensive cologne. Not sweat!

She made her way carefully up the steps, but this time she avoided the rail. If she could survive this miserable little trek, she just might see the inside of the house before the damn sun went down over the "picturesque" mountains looming all around her property.

Not that she appreciated the view. She didn't appreciate anything about this rugged land. She had grown up in a small city, but that was by the sea and huge cites hadn't been far away, especially with an unlimited credit card.

Then when she'd gone to Brown University, she had loved the large population, though she'd been on campus so much and with college life, it was like living in your own personal city with people all your age who shared similar interest. Sighing, she almost wished she could go back…

Back then, she'd already developed the chip on her shoulder when it came to her family, but it hadn't been as bad because she'd loved college, at least at first, and then she'd let the weight of the world settle on her again, and she'd left before she'd graduated. Stupid! That had been stupid.

Had she only finished her degree, she wouldn't be in this mess now, climbing a dilapidated house's front steps with a huge cowboy not far behind her.

"Out here, we're a little more friendly. But it's probably a steep learning curve for a rich bitch like you."

Brielle spun around at the top of the stairs and gazed down at Colt, who was looking up at her with a mocking smile that had her grinding her teeth.

"If I gave a damn about your opinion, I would ask you to speak," she said with what she hoped was a smirk on her lips. There was no way she was going to let this man — this complete stranger — make her day any worse than it already was.

She turned away, but before she had a chance to dig into her purse for the key to the house, she heard the steps creek, and without any more warning than that she *felt* him behind her, making her jump. She faced him again — better to see your enemy — but backed against the door.

He didn't say anything for a few moments, just lowered his face to only inches from her wide-eyed stare.

"Lady, you *really* need to learn basic manners." It wasn't a threat, the voice too low, the sparkle in his eyes telling her he was enjoying himself. But she didn't know this man, didn't know what he was capable of. If she were wise, and at the moment she apparently wasn't, she would apologize and send him away.

But once Brielle felt backed into a corner, she didn't tend to make the wisest of choices. Crew had often told her that when she was a young girl, she would be the first to cut off her own nose just to spite her face. She felt as if she were doing that right now, but she couldn't seem to stop herself from poking the bear — a bear who happened to have some pretty stunning hazel eyes.

When she finally found her voice, she was grateful that it came out with a bite. "Get your hands off me this instant, or I swear you will never be able to have children!"

When he didn't even cringe, just sported a huge grin with perfect white teeth, Brielle tensed, her body preparing to keep the threat she'd just issued. He must have felt her slight movement because suddenly he was pressed up against her, his legs preventing her from lifting her knee.

"Honey, I plan on making lots of babies, so I suggest you don't do that," he practically whispered, making Brielle more furious with her body's reaction to his breath floating across her lips as he dipped his head just a little bit closer.

Utterly, horrifyingly speechless, Brielle found herself looking deep into his eyes, which she was discovering had flecks of silver in them. Why and how could she notice that right now? Shouldn't she be afraid?

"Mmm, Brielle, it's going to be a *pleasure* working with you," he said, leaning even farther forward.

With his lips only half an inch from her own, she sucked her breath in through parted lips, wondering whether she was going to let this stranger — this cowboy — kiss her.

Why in the world would that be the thought crossing her mind? She should be screaming, not contemplating how his lips would feel pressed up against hers. Finally, her voice returned.

"Colt?" The sudden sweetness of her voice must have confused him, because he drew back a few inches, giving her space to breathe.

"Yeah, darlin'?"

"Let's hope you were lying about those babies." The smile she gave him was one of promise.

It took him a moment to process what she was saying, and then he returned her smile with one even brighter than before.

"Again, a pleasure," he said before stepping back, out of kneeing range. "Have a great day."

With those final words, he turned and jumped down the steps, soon disappearing — she didn't know where. After five minutes… ten minutes — hell, maybe an hour — Brielle finally pulled herself from the door and turned around.

That was one hell of a first encounter, and it had started in her first ten minutes on the property. If each day went this well, she wouldn't survive a week…

CHAPTER THREE

He shouldn't have called her a rich bitch. He shouldn't have gotten in her face. He knew he'd made an impression on the city girl, but he might have blown it all with that one careless remark. But she had been acting like a… Nope. Better not even think the word again. There was just too much at stake. His frown deepened as he looked around at the land that should have been his.

It was adjacent to his own ranch, and Arnold had promised him first option on buying the property when the old guy's time came. But Arnold's wife hadn't, and Arnold had gone first. What was it with women?

Colt wanted to expand his 30,000-acre ranch, but Martin Whitman's property sat to his right and there was no chance that man would part with a single acre of his spread. Nor would Colt ever expect him to.

But Arnold's property was ideal. And it was supposed to be his, dammit. When Colt found out that Richard Storm had swooped in and purchased it, he'd been furious. *It was supposed to be his.*

Colt had heard rumors about what was going on in the Storm family. To look at Brielle Storm, it was no wonder — the man's kids were obviously hopeless idiots. And that was a good thing. She was a city girl through and through and had no business running a ranch. No business at all. And that meant that Colt wouldn't have to wait long to get the land.

The world would make sense again.

Or would it? What in the world were those shoes she'd been wearing? Sure, they were red and incredibly sexy, but they weren't for Montana, and certainly not for a Montana ranch. Hell, no! They were more suited for a night on the town, or maybe for the bedroom — just the shoes, with nothing else on...

Nope!

He was thrusting...er...pushing...*removing* that thought right out of his mind. He was there to convince her she wasn't suited to running a ranch, convince her to sell to him. And his task had just become a whole lot easier. The worthless little brat thought he was an employee of hers.

Though Colt hoped he wasn't normally so cruel, even in thought, this woman had immediately burrowed under his skin, and in the wrong places. She's just been so...stuck-up — or maybe something was stuck up her sweet backside — and she obviously had no justification for her arrogance. But the babe didn't want to be here, so they could both win if he bought her out. He hated deceiving her, for even a short time, as he wasn't usually dishonest. He'd grown up in the tiny town of Sterling, Montana, population negative two, he thought with a soft chuckle, and around here, neighbors were...well, neighborly. It was a tight-knit community, and they all helped each other, no matter what needed to be done.

Yes, there was more money floating through this section of Montana than they held at Fort Knox, but no one was arrogant; no one had a superiority complex. They might make megabucks off the rich land filled with good fields, healthy livestock, and oil — actually, good investments in the stock market had played a larger part for many of them — but at the end of the day, all they needed was a cold beer and a hot fire.

Colt's idea of heaven was lounging around on the edge of his lake with a fishing pole, a cold bottle in his hand and his hat pulled low over his eyes. Once nighttime hit, of course, he didn't mind having a fine body — like the one Brielle was sporting — to climb on top of him and take him for much longer than an eight-second ride.

Colt knew he could draw in the ladies. Hell, he'd learned that in second grade, when little Sally had come up and kissed him right on the lips and begged him to run away with her. He'd been horrified.

Then.

Now, well, now he just appreciated a fine woman on top *or* beneath him — either way, he didn't mind. Or side to side, or standing up, or... He was equal opportunity all the way. And he *always* made sure the women in his bed left with a smile on their faces and him on their mind.

He wasn't ready to settle down. Hell, he'd only just turned thirty-three. Who could possibly object to his bachelor life?

Okay, he knew three people who seemed to object mighty loudly. Those women! The terrible trio! Maggie, Eileen, and the worst one of all, Bethel!

They were somewhere in their sixties, he believed, not that anyone knew for sure, as the women didn't speak of their age. They acted more like teenagers than grandmothers. Though he had a soft spot in his heart for each one of them, lately he and all the other single men in town had been running as fast as they could away from the three.

Those meddlers clearly wanted to see all the eligible men married and producing babies. Not for him — not yet, at least. Colt had done a damn fine job of steering clear of the trio, because every time they saw him they mentioned all the attractive single women around. It didn't do a man any good to date a woman in Sterling, because sure as the sun rose every morning, the minute that happened, the poor sap would be heading down the aisle within a year.

That's what was expected here. First comes love…and then a whole brood of rug rats biting your ankles and playing havoc with your sleep.

He hadn't really meant what he'd said about making a lot of babies, but when he'd pressed up against Brielle, she had sent a surge of lust ripping through him that he hadn't experienced since he was sixteen and Margie Thomas had thrust her newly developed breasts against him in the locker room. Damn, the feeling he'd felt with Brielle had been even stronger. And Colt hadn't ever thought that was possible. No. But anyway, he had a few good decades in him before any woman made a fool out of him and his sperm.

He almost swaggered into the large horse barn on Brielle's property. He knew he'd find her foreman, Tony, coddling the horses. Tony had worked on the Ponderosa Pines Ranch since before Colt was born. What little hair the man had left was now completely white, but his skin was leathery and his body was slim.

"Hello, Colt," Tony said with his typical scowl. "What are you doing out here?" A stranger would consider Tony intimidating, but Colt knew that beneath the gruffness, the man had a heart of gold. He was a big baby when it came to kids, little old women, and newborn animals. Tony didn't smile much, but when he did, even more wrinkles appeared around his eyes and mouth.

"You know I had to show up and check out my competition," Colt said with a laugh.

"What did you think?" Tony asked.

"Ha." Colt didn't elaborate. He stepped up on the rail and stood next to Tony as they looked out at the men training a new horse that Arnold's widow, Candice, had bought right before she passed away.

"Aw, hell, Colt. No city girl will know how to run a ranch. It won't be long before she sprints out of here crying, and then the land's all yours," Tony said with his version of a chuckle. Then he turned his head and spit out a long stream of tobacco-colored saliva.

"Yeah. Well, I still wanted to meet her." Colt remembered the shock in her almost translucent green eyes. Shaking his head to clear it, he turned back to Tony just in time to catch his friend's words.

"What's she like?"

"Exactly what we expected, Tony. A city girl, one who showed up in tight jeans with sparkly little jewels on the ass so every man has no choice but to look down, and a silk blouse that will be destroyed by the end of one day here in the country. Red hair, and even redder high heels, and those fancy nails city girls like to wear. I don't think she's ever so much as rinsed her own plate before."

"Yeah. That's what I thought." Tony turned back toward the horse just in time to see him rear up on his hind legs in all his glory.

"He sure is a beauty," Colt said with a low whistle as the ranch hand got the horse to settle back down and began walking him in circles through the training ring.

"Yeah, he is. That was a good move on Candice's part. I just wish she'd stayed with us long enough to ride him one time."

"Yeah. This one is taking a lot longer to train. I hate that he was abused."

"He's doing much better now. The hands have been working with him a little bit more each week. It won't be long now," Tony said with no little pride.

Tony had more patience than most people could ever dream of, but when he did finally lose his temper, watch out. He might have been getting up there in years, but it wasn't his fault the Ponderosa Pines Ranch had been failing. Arnold and Candice had just run out of funds, and instead of asking a bank for help, they kept silent, making Tony do the same.

By the time Candice had departed the world, the ranch was in serious need of cash and an owner who was willing to invest time and effort into replanting the wheat, bringing in more cattle, and doing much-needed repairs.

When Richard Storm had shown up and scooped up the property, Colt had been surprised and then furious, in part because no outsider could give the Ponderosa Pines what she needed. But at least Richard had ensured that Tony would stay on by increasing his pay. Richard had also asked the foreman to see that his daughter learned how to run a ranch.

Colt had just so happened to be in on that meeting and he'd ended up walking out. Raising Richard's child wasn't Tony's job. Tony had laughed at the request, though. He'd seen city girls come to Montana before. Then he'd watched them leave quicker than a tornado that had destroyed all it was prepared to destroy.

Brielle Storm would be no different. Colt didn't give the girl a single week of ranch life before she was begging him to buy the land.

"Brielle thinks I work for her."

It took a couple of moments before Tony's lips turned up. Then he was laughing outright. At first, Colt was in shock, but he couldn't help but join in the laughter.

"Well, don't that just work to your advantage?" Tony asked when he was done chuckling.

The ranch hand in the ring with the horse turned their way and stared for a minute before getting back to what he was doing. When Tony laughed, it did tend to stop traffic, considering it was more of a coughing spasm than real laughter.

"Yeah. It does," Colt replied. "Make sure you tell the hands not to give anything away — not that I expect her to speak much to them, if she speaks to them at all. I got the impression she thinks she is far above any of us rednecks out here in Montana." He lowered his voice and intensified the drawl.

"Yeah, people who aren't from around here tend to judge us pretty quickly. Let them make all the assumptions they want. You know that only makes them the *ass* of our jokes."

"All right. I better head home. Jackson is stopping by later for a beer." Colt didn't bother sticking out his hand. Tony didn't shake them — not ever.

Climbing down from the rail, Colt strolled from the barn with a whistle on his lips and plans in his head for what he was going to do to improve this property once it was in his hands. It was early June now, so the wheat crop would soon be growing high, and as the weather was cooperating so far, by late July or early August the fields would be ready to harvest. He hoped it was his land by then.

Without a care in the world, Colt walked to where he'd left his horse, climbed on, and made his way at full speed toward his beautiful spread and sprawling ranch house. This was going to be another very good year for him.

At least that's what he thought…

CHAPTER FOUR

"CREW! I DON'T have time for this. I'm in way over my head, have no idea what I'm doing, and to top all of that off, I was attacked yesterday by a monster of a man!"

"What?"

Finally, she'd managed to say something that was getting her brother's attention. She'd been on the phone with him for the past half hour, furious with her father, with having to be in Montana, and just plain annoyed with the way her life was going.

"At least *that* got your attention. This man who showed up slightly after I arrived here was rude, snarky, and had the nerve to call me a rich bitch. Then he trapped me against the house — well, sort of trapped me. He didn't actually touch me...no, scratch that, he did press against me when I threatened him, but the point is that this guy, this *Colt*..." Brielle said the name like a swear word before continuing. "He's one of my employees. How the hell do I deal with that?"

The steam died down as she finished speaking. She hadn't exactly felt *threatened*, but that wasn't the point. The point was... She didn't really know the point. She just needed to vent, and Crew was a willing ear to vent to. Though she didn't realize it, her father's plan *was* working.

Even though she hadn't forgiven her father, and had only spoken to him when she absolutely had to, she was uniting with her brother again, reaching out to him, and asking for advice.

"Um...sis. That doesn't exactly sound like you were attacked."

"Oh, what would you know? You don't even care. I actually called you for advice, and all you've done is mock me."

"That's not true," he said and a hush fell between them. "Look, Brielle. I know we've drifted apart. I know I haven't been there for you, but I have to tell you, this year has..." He had to search for the right words before continuing. "It's just been an eye-opener. At first I hated Dad. Hated what he was doing, hated that he was controlling us. But I realize now that he has given us a gift," he said with another long sigh. "Don't you dare tell the old man I said that, though!"

"Like I'm ever speaking to him again!"

"Brielle, you *will* get over the horror. I was feeling just as bad as you when I got to Catalina, but now I find myself taking pride in what I'm doing. Dad was right. We were getting pretty entitled. It's felt good to work with my hands again, just like I used to when I was a teen."

"Oh, what would you know? You're in sunny California — on a resort on a freaking island. I'm in the backwoods of Montana. Two entirely different situations."

"Aw, Montana will grow on you," he assured her.

"What about the money? I told you about the ridiculously little bit I have."

"I made my budget work. You can do it. Just no fancy clothes or salons."

"You never did understand me, Crew Storm, or why I do what I do. The only nice clothes I have are now more than a year out of season — I sold off what I could. And I hate you," she said, but without any heat.

"I miss you, Brielle."

That stopped her short. She couldn't remember the last time one of her brothers had said those words to her. She found her throat tight with emotion, but she absolutely refused to show such a weakness to her big brother. She fell silent until she got herself under control.

"Well, since you aren't being any help at all, Crew, I'm going to try to figure this out on my own. I guess I have a foreman who runs things around here."

"That's a start. Keep me updated on what you're doing."

"Fine. But only so you know how miserable I am," she said, unwilling to admit to him that she missed him, too. If she admitted that, she would have to think about the past, think about what had torn them apart in the first place, and that was a place she never wanted to revisit again.

"I'll speak to you soon, Peaches."

Before she was able to snap at him about that damn nickname, he hung up the phone. The thing was that she wasn't angry about hearing it now, just a little sad that it had been lost in the first place. What was this place doing to her? She didn't even know who in the hell she was anymore, let alone what she was going to do next. She was supposed to be here for a full year at a minimum. She'd never survive it.

Returning her vulnerability to the shelf in the back of her mind, Brielle decided it was time to find her foreman. She was going to do what she had to do and then she was getting as far from this stupid state as she possibly could.

Hell, maybe she'd even leave the country once her trust fund was back in place. That thought should have made her smile. It didn't. Everything seemed to make her feel empty these days.

But then Colt appeared in her head. There had been nothing empty about what that man had made her feel in the few minutes they'd been together.

Sick! That thought appalled her, so she left the house and began walking. Ready or not, her foreman was about to find out just how stubborn Brielle could be.

CHAPTER FIVE

"WHAT DO YOU mean, 'no'?" Brielle thundered at the man standing before her.

All he did was let loose with a long stream of spit that nearly landed on her toes. She squealed and jumped back.

"Do you realize that these are three-*thousand*-dollar Jimmy Choo shoes?" she gasped.

"Yeah. I figured they were some ridiculous amount, and they certainly shouldn't be worn in a horse barn," Tony said before spitting again.

"Well, that's not your concern now, is it?"

"I don't really give a damn what you wear," he told her, then turned and walked away.

"You *work* for me!" Brielle yelled at his back, but her words didn't even slow his pace. She found herself chasing after her foreman once again.

"I've got work to do, ma'am. I don't have time to coddle you." Tony moved into his office at the back of the barn.

She hated this room, hated how bad it smelled, and hated how cluttered it was. Still, she never complained about his space, because if it weren't for this man, she'd be totally screwed. No doubt about it. Not that Tony listened to her. None of the men did. Including the first ranch hand she'd met on the very first day she was here. What was his name again? Colt. Like she'd really forgotten…

Two weeks she'd been there, and yes, she'd admit that she'd been less than pleasant at first, but the last few days she'd decided she was stuck, and she was through being bored. After speaking with Crew just now, she really wanted to prove she could do this.

She'd even watched about two dozen cowboy films this last week — wouldn't that help her learn something about ranching? So far, though, she knew she was falling very short of what she was supposed to be doing.

"Listen, Tony. I think we've just gotten off on the wrong foot. How about we start over and be friends?" She gave him her most winning smile.

Tony looked up and gave some sort of movement to his lips that she supposed could be considered a smile, and she thought for sure that she'd finally won him over until a shadow fell over her and the room seemed to shrink.

Nope. Tony's smile, or whatever it could be called, wasn't for her. It was for the man standing behind her. And she knew exactly who it was. Not because she'd seen him yet, but because she could *feel* him.

"Afternoon, Tony. Problems?" Colt asked as he walked up beside Brielle.

She did her best not to look at him. If that happened, she'd lose her breath and get all airheaded. She wasn't an airheaded type of girl. Yes, there were some people who might think that about her, but it was far from true. She'd actually been a straight-A student in high school and during her first year of college.

She'd made it into Brown, after all. Did these guys have any idea how much of an accomplishment that was? They had only a 9 percent acceptance rate for undergraduate applicants.

Perhaps her major hadn't been the most practical: she'd studied English. But if anyone thought that was easy, far from it. She'd worked her tail off, and she'd planned on going into journalism, and working for a paper or magazine at some point. No, things didn't end up working out, but it wasn't over yet.

She'd ended up mixing with some people who partied hard after that first year, and fallen off a bit, but when she'd slipped up in a few classes, she'd manned back up and done better the next year. Everyone might think she didn't have a care in the world, but she did take pride in accomplishing a difficult task. She would finish her degree!

But she'd never imagined she'd be doing something as difficult as running a ranch, especially when no one at the Ponderosa Pines Ranch would allow her to do anything involving the day-to-day operations. It wasn't as if she could fire them all and start over.

She wouldn't even know where to begin. She couldn't say she want to wrestle around with the few livestock they had, or mend the fences, but she did want to see how it operated, wanted to understand it, wanted to know why it was failing, and how she could turn it around.

If she was stuck in this place for an entire year, then she was going to walk away with at least some knowledge. She might not like that her father had thrown this at her, but she had accepted the challenge. Still, that wouldn't stop her from grabbing her calendar and marking off each day she was trapped here.

"The little woman here wants someone to take her out on the land," Tony said, rolling his eyes in disbelief.

"And there's nothing wrong with that," Brielle said. What sort of a chauvinist was he? "Tony just said *no*. He didn't explain why, just told me *no*." She lifted her head and met Colt's gaze.

Dammit. It had taken only about thirty seconds before she was making eye contact. The man really did muddle her brain. She seriously wanted to stamp her feet. But she was trying to grow here, and throwing a tantrum was the opposite of growth.

So Brielle just stood there, hating that her eyes were pleading for one of the two men to listen to her. She needed to inspect her property.

At least that's what her brother Crew had told her to do. And since Crew was all happy with his project and kicking ass at it, she'd decided she'd better listen and check out the land she now owned.

Her father had called several times and left messages, but she was still angry with him and had refused to take his calls, refused to call him back. Let him sweat. She hoped he was worried that wild coyotes were going to drag her off into the hills at any minute. Wait. That thought stopped her cold.

"There aren't wild coyotes who eat people here, are there?" she asked, and felt like a fool when both men grinned.

"Not usually," Colt said, the start of a chuckle evident in his throat, though he was doing his best to keep his mirth at bay.

She wanted to imitate her last name and storm from the barn. The only thing that stopped her was that she knew both men would be a whole hell of a lot happier if she did just that. Well, tough. She wasn't going anywhere.

"Again, I want to explore my land. I need to know why the operation is failing. Who is going to take me?"

This time Brielle faced Tony with her shoulders back and a determined glint in her eyes. She wasn't going to back down again, even if he did intimidate the hell out of her.

This time, she was going to get her way, and she was going to learn something about all these acres of land she'd unwillingly inherited from her father. She would make this damn ranch successful even if it killed her. And it might just.

"I'll take you," Colt said, surprising not only her but Tony as well, if his expression was any indication.

"You sure you have time for that, Colt?" Tony asked, making Brielle want to slug him.

"Yeah. I've got my projects done for the day," he said with a shrug before turning back to her. "But there's no way you're getting on a horse wearing that ensemble. You need to change into jeans and boots. A hat wouldn't hurt either. It will shield your face from the sun."

"I don't need fashion advice from a cowboy." What was wrong with the cute shorts and tank top she was wearing? It was an unusually warm summer, she'd been told. And that was okay with her. She loved hot weather, and she hadn't gotten enough of it in Maine.

"I'm not giving you fashion advice, Princess. I'm just stating how it is. You'll break your neck if you even attempt to get on a horse in those heels. And your thighs will be scraped raw if you wear shorts on the long ride."

Colt leaned against the wall and crossed one foot in front of the other, his thumbs tucked into his front pockets. He looked as if he could stand right there all day long and not be bothered in the least.

"Well, I don't have that sort of clothes," she said with a frustrated sigh.

The thing she wouldn't admit to either man was that she was excited to take her first horseback ride. She'd seen it done in the movies all the time, and it actually looked like fun. But if she told them that, they'd just ramp up the mockery. She was through with being pegged as the dumb city girl.

"We'll have to hit Peggy's shop, and then I'll take you out," Colt said as he pushed off the wall and moved to the door. He turned around before he walked through it. "I'll see ya later, Tony."

With that, he left the room. Brielle stood there for a minute, watching his retreat through the open doorway. She knew he expected her to follow him without question.

The stubborn Storm blood in her told her to stand her ground. After all, *she* was the boss here. But the practical part of her told her that he didn't give a damn. If she didn't follow him, she'd lose her tour guide.

Curiosity and a desire to ride the land made her decision for her. She turned to follow him, but still stopped in the doorway and turned to give Tony a narrow-eyed glance. "We *will* talk further."

He just stared back at her with surprisingly alert brown eyes. The man was wrinkled, balding, scrawny, and downright rude, but she had a feeling nothing got past him. She couldn't fire him. That would be foolish.

"Looking forward to it," Tony finally said before setting his hat back on his head and standing up.

She knew he was getting ready to leave the room too, so she decided to make her exit first. It was a matter of pride. Spinning around, she walked away feeling as if she'd just had a small victory. A smile even tilted the corners of her lips, if just the smallest fraction of an inch. But it was still a smile.

By the time her ride ended, that smile would be long gone.

CHAPTER SIX

DEAD SILENCE WAS their companion as Brielle rode in the shotgun seat of Colt's huge diesel pickup truck. The black beast boasted more bells and whistles inside the cab than her last Mercedes had.

How could a ranch hand afford such a smooth ride?

It was killing her not to ask him, but she refused to. She'd be damned if she spoke first. No way. No how! Brielle Storm was used to having people cater to *her* needs. That had been the story of her life. Well, it had been the story of her life up until a year ago, when her father had pulled her sweet Persian rug right out from under her.

Now she was twenty-five, living in a slightly ramshackle home, owner of a failing 10,000-acre ranch, and in charge of a whole hell of a lot of men who wouldn't even look at her, let alone listen to a word she said. This was not something Brielle was used to, and it wasn't something she planned to ever get used to.

Still, she was finally getting somewhere today. She was going to inspect her property, learn what ranching was all about, and when she did see her father, she wouldn't sound like a twit. After all, the stars of all those cowboy flicks she'd watched made ranching look easy — well, when they didn't end up in one mishap or other, that is.

She was too smart to make a fool of herself, so she had nothing to worry about, did she?

The truck cruised down the long Montana road without her feeling a bump. It was a much different ride than the one she'd approached the house in. Why had her father bought that old and rusty truck? Was that part of her punishment? She was sure it was. He had to be sitting back in his nice, comfy office chair with a cigar in his mouth and a grin on his face as he thought about his spoiled daughter fighting the elements and who knew what else in Montana.

When they pulled off the roadway and Colt suddenly swung in front of a store that simply said *Peggy's* in big bold red letters, Brielle looked up and down the street. Surely this couldn't be Sterling.

Could it?

She was seeing a post office, a very *small* post office, a pharmacy, a dental office, a sheriff's office, maybe a salon, and a small café. There were a few other small buildings scattered on the street, and what looked to be a fire station not far away, but this one little street just couldn't be the town she was expected to live in for the next year.

Her throat was practically burning with her need to talk, but she was still unwilling to speak first. She couldn't! But when Colt climbed wordlessly from the truck and moved around to her side of the vehicle and opened the door, she was unable to take it any longer.

"Where are we?" she practically shouted, clearly startling him with the decibel level of her voice.

"Sterling," he answered as he held out a hand to help her down.

Ignoring the hand he was offering, she grabbed the handle above her and stepped onto the wide running board before landing on the sidewalk next to Colt.

"This isn't the whole town, though, is it?" Please, please, *please* don't be the whole town, she added silently.

"You're looking at the town center," he drawled, and she practically wept with relief until he continued. "Around the corner sits the school, and ball fields, and two churches. Then Sterling stretches for miles in each direction. We're a ranching community with lots of cattle, wheat, and oil. We don't need a whole heck of a lot of shops."

"But there are more stores than this, right?" This was what she wanted to know.

"Nope. This is it."

"This can't be it!" She began walking, reached the end of the street in less than a minute, and then spun on her heels and headed the other way, passing Colt where he was still standing next to his truck, leaning against the side as if he had all day to wait for her. Of course he could lean like that — it wouldn't take her long at all to traverse the entire town!

Brielle moved to the other end of the pathetic "main street" and looked out to see some houses dotted along the next street over, along with the school and churches he'd just mentioned, and that was it. Colt hadn't been duping her. This one street, one simple street, contained every freaking business in the tiny town.

She found that the place she'd thought was a hair salon was proudly announcing in their window that they did nails. Then there was what looked like a *Little House on the Prairie* sort of store, and a grocery store with a huge neon Coors Light sign blinking in the front window.

She really was in hell. No, this was worse than hell. At least in hell a person could find evidence of exciting vices, but none of those could be seen in this pitiful excuse for a place. She felt totally defeated.

"How far away is the nearest *real* town?" she asked when she reached Colt again.

"Sterling *is* a real town."

His chuckle made her want to claw his eyes out.

"Okay, how far is it to find the nearest *large* town?" Why, oh why hadn't she done some research, any at all, on where she was going? Probably because she hadn't planned on staying, and probably because she'd never have figured that a town this small actually existed.

"Well, Billings is about half an hour's drive away."

"I want to go there for clothes." Brielle indicated that she'd like for him to move from the passenger door so she could climb back into his truck. She expected nothing less than his full compliance. He did work for her, after all.

"Too bad" was all he said. He clicked the lock button on his key fob and headed toward Peggy's.

Brielle was so stunned that she didn't move from her place on the surprisingly pristine sidewalk for a full thirty seconds. "Oh, this is *so* my last straw," she muttered as her eyes narrowed and she took determined steps in his direction.

She was through with cowboys, through with Sterling, and through with this business of ranching. Someone was damn well going to listen to her today — and that someone just happened to be Colt Westbrook.

Fury rolling off her in waves, she practically took the glass door off its hinges when she barreled into Peggy's clothing store. When she came up against a solid wall of muscled chest, she didn't slow down; she just plowed into him with such force that she knocked him off balance, causing them both to go sailing toward the floor.

All the air was ripped from Brielle's lungs when she landed on Colt's chest, her breasts bouncing off him before she settled in and found herself pressed tightly against his body.

Once the shock wore off, a new light entered his eyes — a light Brielle didn't want to think about. She knew that look, knew exactly what was on his mind. No flipping way.

Too late.

"If you wanted to get me horizontal, all you had to do was ask."

That was all the warning Brielle got before Colt gripped the back of her neck and pulled her face to his, then gave her the most searing kiss of her life.

Peggy's store, and the entire town of Sterling, disappeared in a single heartbeat.

CHAPTER SEVEN

"HELLO, COLT. LOOKING for something?"

Damn. Damn. Damn. It was just getting good. Colt wasn't happy to release a now horrified Brielle, but the viselike grip he'd had around her waist loosened and she scrambled to her feet as if he were a teeming anthill.

"Morning, Peggy," he said, not bothering to get up quite yet. Instead, he flipped his hands behind his head and grinned up at the shop's owner as she scowled down at him.

"This store isn't your personal brothel, Colt." One foot was tapping while she rested her hands on her ample hips.

"Aw, Peggy, I just got carried away. What else was I supposed to do when a hot little number like Brielle comes hurtling through your doors and literally knocks me off my feet?" he asked, amping up the wattage on his killer smile.

"When that happens, what you *should* do is help the lady back up on her feet and then do some shopping — a *lot* of shopping."

"That's what we're planning on doing, darlin'. And as you can see, she had no problem getting up all on her own." Okay, it was probably time to get up off the floor.

The store wasn't huge, but somehow Brielle had managed to disappear, and he figured it was about time to find her. Sparks were flying between them, and though he knew it wasn't a good idea to pursue the enemy, he couldn't seem to talk himself out of it. Ms. Storm intrigued him.

That hoity-toity image she'd assumed and wanted him to think she was all about had to be a smoke screen, because the kiss she'd just given back to him was about as hot as it got. There were some serious fireworks hidden inside Brielle, and she'd just ignited his curiosity — and that wasn't all she'd ignited. The home fires were burning.

Halfway to the back of the store, where the women's clothing was located, Colt got distracted by a rack holding new merchandise. He could use a few more shirts. Having no qualms about stripping in the store, he began unbuttoning the shirt he was wearing, pulled it from his broad shoulders, and flung it over a chair.

He didn't notice Brielle stopping in her tracks as she came around a clothing rack and focused in on his obscenely toned abs. Working on the land day and night had done delectable things for his body, and Brielle was openmouthed and wide-eyed, with her gaze locked in tight on his midsection.

When Colt turned and saw the look she was sending his way, he stopped what he was doing, which left him standing there with one sleeve of the shirt on and one not, and with his bare chest on display for anyone who happened to stroll into the store.

After a few tense seconds, Colt broke out into a grin, looked down at her luscious pink lips, and took a step toward her. That startled her enough to make eye contact with him. *Perfect.*

"Enjoying the view, Princess?" he asked with an exaggerated drawl.

"Just trying to figure out if you're as arrogant as you act. I guess you are."

Colt might have been offended, but that look in her eyes was pure fire. He'd seen it before, so he wasn't fooled — not at all. She wanted him, and if he put in the slightest bit of effort, he had no doubt that she'd be his. Colt just had to choose whether he wanted to make that happen or not.

He decided right then and there that he was going to find out.

A plan in place, Colt slid the shirt the rest of the way on and buttoned it up, then turned to find the mirror. "Nice color. Pull the tag, Peggy. I'll wear this one home."

"You're going to need to buy a few more things before you're forgiven for your previous display, Colt Westbrook!" But Peggy was already thawing as she moved toward Brielle. There was nothing Peggy liked more than to outfit a pretty lady — and Brielle was certainly that.

Colt couldn't wait to see what the newcomer looked like in some cowgirl wear. Shopping wasn't one of his favorite pastimes, but playing hooky from his ranch for an afternoon was probably worth it in this case.

"Come on, honey," Peggy said, taking Brielle's arm. "Let's find you some real clothes. I don't know where you did your shopping before now, but those clothes, and especially those shoes, will land you with nothing but a broken ankle on top of a bad sunburn." Now that Peggy wasn't distracted by Colt, she went back into merchant mode.

Brielle turned toward Colt with a look of panic in her eyes, but he just tipped his hat and smiled. He'd been the enemy just a few seconds earlier, but now the woman was looking to him to save her.

This was one mission he didn't want to rescue her from. He wanted to see her all dressed up and ready to ranch. Not that he had any faith that the clothes would suddenly change her, make her an instant cowgirl. But in the space of a few minutes, he was thinking that city girls might not be so bad after all.

No. He had no business thinking that. Sure, he might want to play with the city girl, but at the end of the day he wanted her long gone from his neck of the woods — far away, with only memories left from her stay in Montana.

She was on his land, dammit, and he would get it back. No matter what it took, he was going to have her on the first plane out of Sterling that he possibly could. Still, the two of them might just have to play a little bit before that one-way flight.

Taking his time about it, he found her and Peggy at a rack of Wrangler jeans. "I think these will be a perfect fit," Peggy was saying as she pulled out a pair that looked as if they would be show Brielle's fine ass to perfection.

He joined the conversation enthusiastically. "I agree."

"Colt may act like an ass," Peggy said, echoing one word of his thoughts, "but he does have good taste when it comes to clothing. You should listen to him." Her sugary-sweet sales voice had Colt in yet another of his patented grins.

Brielle's enthusiasm didn't match Colt's.

She was soon being pushed from one rack of clothes to the next, and her arms were laden with things she knew she'd never wear again after she left this benighted place. She didn't want to even think about the money she was about to spend on clothes that she would have scoffed at before today. Heck, she was *still* scoffing today.

When she finally made it to the changing room and slipped into a pair of the jeans and a button-down shirt, she felt itchy and uncomfortable. She was used to silk and cashmere, not cotton and polyester. She'd never get used to this new life. But if she wanted to earn the respect of the men working for her, she needed to fit in to their world a little better.

Even if it would kill her budget. She hoped her father would mellow out before too much longer, and maybe, just maybe, let her have access to her trust fund again. Maybe she'd better quit ignoring his calls if she hoped for that to happen. This shopping trip wouldn't make the slightest dent in the money she had sitting in her frozen bank account.

Just the thought of her old platinum credit card made her want to cry. There was a time she hadn't had to think about the cost of anything. Now, a fifty-dollar pair of jeans was making her break out in a sweat.

One thing she was learning from all of this was that she should be a lot more grateful for what she'd had. Not everyone lived the way she used to live, and not everyone was just handed everything. But that was probably one of the lessons her father wanted to teach her and her brothers.

Slipping into the boots that Colt had picked out for her, she looked at her reflection in the full-length mirror and grimaced to see herself in such an outfit. No way could she pull this off. She just wasn't made to be a ranch girl. She was made to live in the city in a nice safe condo where someone else did the yard work. That was just who she was. The sooner everyone in her life accepted that, the sooner she could get back to the real world. Her real world.

"Come out, Brielle," Colt said. "I know it can't take that long to change, not even for a princess."

She glared at the curtain separating her from Colt, but she had no doubt he would barge in on her if she didn't comply. The sad thing was that the thought of him sharing the small dressing room with her wasn't as horrifying as it should have been, not after that burning kiss. She feared she'd be replaying that several nights in a row in her dreams.

"I'm coming. Keep your pants on." She pulled the curtain back and stepped out. "I don't see how you people can deal with these clothes. My toes feel as if they're being crushed." She twirled around as a joke. This wasn't a fashion show she'd ever thought she'd participate in — that was for damn sure.

Colt stepped up behind her when her twirl left her back facing him. His hands slid around the curve of her hips and his thumbs settled in her front pockets as he turned their bodies so he could look into her light green eyes through the full-length mirror.

"I think you look pretty damn hot in this outfit," he whispered against her ear, letting his lips brush the tender flesh of her neck as he bent just a little lower. "And these jeans have the added advantage of being the perfect resting place for a man's hands." He let his fingertips graze the top of her thighs.

Where was Peggy when Brielle needed someone to run interference? The shopkeeper had suddenly disappeared, and no one else seemed to be in the store. Gulping, Brielle knew she was in trouble, because she couldn't find one single comeback to Colt's lines.

She remained motionless as he kept pressing against her. What this man was doing to her body should be against the law. If someone had told her last year that she'd be melting into a giant puddle over a ranch hand, she would have given out a ladylike guffaw. Right now, however, she didn't feel in the least like laughing.

When he finally let her go, she walked almost in a trance back into the changing room, pulled the curtain back into place, slowly unbuttoned the shirt, and let it float to the floor. Then she just stood there looking into the mirror at her flushed cheeks.

This man was clearly making her appearance change. If the glow in her eyes had anything to do with something other than Colt Westbrook, she didn't know what it could be. It certainly wasn't the crisp Montana air.

When the curtain parted and Colt was suddenly standing behind her again, Brielle didn't even try to act as if she didn't want him there. Since that first kiss on the shop floor, she'd been waiting for the next.

To hell with what she *should* be doing. She wanted to taste him again, wanted to feel the lightning flash across her skin. No, she wasn't a virgin, but she couldn't ever recall wanting a man so badly. It wasn't as if she'd been with a dozen men — only two, in fact. But she had a rising suspicion that Colt was going to be the third.

That thought should have caused her some anxiety, but as she turned and his arms wrapped around her, all she could feel were burning embers traveling to her core.

"You are a devil in disguise," Colt murmured, and took her mouth in a kiss that was far from gentle.

CHAPTER EIGHT

WHEN SHE EMERGED from the changing room, Brielle knew she looked as if she'd just had sex. They hadn't — of course not! — but she wasn't a fool. Her hair was mussed, her lips red and swollen, and that certainly wasn't cosmetic blusher on her cheeks.

No. Sadly enough, a man hadn't been able to put this sort of glow in her face in too long to remember. Maybe ever, actually. She was used to being with controlled men, men who asked permission before they kissed her.

She'd thought that was what she wanted. But apparently she'd been a bit wrong, because right now all she could think about was darting back into that changing room, ripping Colt's clothes off, and finishing what the two of them had started.

Closing her eyes, she ran through the past ten minutes again and again in her head. The feel of his strong hands moving slowly up and down her back, the way his lips had parted hers, and how his tongue had slipped inside her mouth.

When he'd gripped her backside and lifted her up against him, she'd nearly come right then and there just from feeling his hardness. This man was lethal, but she couldn't seem to tell herself to back away.

She wanted to be with him, wanted to have his hands all over her, and wanted to keep tasting his kisses. She wanted a lot more from Colt Westbrook. Why even try to run?

This would stop, she assured herself. She just needed some air. When she looked up, grateful he was giving her five feet of space, she found her eyes fastening on a set of three elderly ladies who were slack-jawed and sparkly-eyed.

"I don't think we've had the pleasure of meeting, darling," one of the women said as they all stepped forward. "I'm Bethel, and these two women here are my friends, Eileen and Maggie." She pointed first to one and then the other.

Brielle was at a loss for words for a few seconds as she struggled to switch off her lustful thoughts and focus on the women in front of her. She had best get used to strangers introducing themselves in this town, because it seemed that no one was looked at as a stranger here.

She accepted the hand that Bethel was holding out and said, "I'm Brielle Storm."

"Ah. You're the new owner at the Ponderosa Pines Ranch," Bethel said, and the other two women nodded knowingly.

"So, we see you're here with Colt," one of the other women said — was it Eileen or Maggie? Damn! — and the smile she sent Brielle's way started to make her really nervous. She didn't know why, but it seemed as if these women were analyzing her, maybe planning something, something she was sure she wanted no part of. Shifting on her feet, she tried to figure out the best escape route possible, but there seemed to be nowhere to run.

"Yes, he brought me here to get some work clothes. I…um…wasn't quite prepared for the ranch," Brielle admitted, amazed when she felt her cheeks redden even more.

She was a Storm, and at one time even the mention of her name had brought a reverent silence. Money talked. But she didn't have any now, and there was no sign of either reverence or silence from the three women standing before her.

"Ladies, are you giving Brielle a hard time?"

Suddenly, Colt was standing next to her, his arm slung across her back. Of course, the three women's eyes zeroed in on the protective gesture. Brielle tried to squirm away, but he was strong *and* determined, and without doing some all-too-obvious twisting, she wasn't going to escape his hold.

"Not at all, Colt. We were just introducing ourselves. Martin's over at the café and he said the two of you came in here about an hour ago,"

Eileen said with a sly smile. "We were just wondering why picking out a few items of clothing was taking so long."

"And now we know," Maggie said, offering her own sly glance at Colt's hand, which was resting just above Brielle's hip.

As if finally getting clued in to what these women were up to, and where their eyes were, he untangled himself from Brielle and put a good three feet of space between them.

"Brielle didn't have proper clothes for riding or ranching. We've just been shopping." Colt's cheeks seemed to gain instant color to match Brielle's.

"That's not what we've been hearing. Peggy said you were assisting Brielle in the changing room," Bethel said.

Brielle was mortified to discover that people had been paying attention. Peggy hadn't been anywhere in sight when Colt had slipped in there with her. But *of course* the woman knew what was happening in her own store. What had Brielle been thinking when she allowed that make-out session to go on in such a public place? Okay, maybe she wasn't all that surprised at what she'd done. And she couldn't regret it altogether. His kisses were *that* good.

She was, however, more than a little uncomfortable now that she was being examined under a high-powered microscope. Were these women finding her seriously lacking? They probably didn't think her good enough for one of their own small-town cowboys.

That thought stung, though it shouldn't have. She knew who she was and what she was worth. But that was just it. She didn't really know who she was. She knew she was a Storm, but that didn't mean anything anymore, and certainly nothing in this town. She felt as if she were floating on a cloud and she just didn't know when it was going to start dropping rain, leaving a big hole for her to fall through.

"We don't want to be a bother," Maggie said. "We just wanted to meet Brielle and see what you've been up to, Colt. It seems you've been avoiding us lately."

"Why would I ever avoid you three beautiful women?"

"Oh, don't even try that on us, Colt Westbrook," Bethel told him. "Or that ridiculous smile. We're not some dumb young girls who can be fooled by your charm. If your mama was still alive, she'd be crying in her favorite front-porch rocking chair right about now, complaining about what a playboy you've become."

"My mama raised me right, ladies," he said, tipping his hat and looking around for a way out. When the doorbell rang and a man walked in, Colt's face filled with relief. "I would love to keep chatting, but I need to speak to Hawk." And he made a beeline for him, a man who didn't know the minefield he was stepping into.

The new arrival made Brielle's jaw drop. "Do they grow them all to be tall, dark and handsome here?" she couldn't help asking.

"I think it's something in the water," Bethel replied with a laugh.

"Nah, it's the sweet-corn whiskey," Eileen argued.

"That's my son, Hawk. He's the local fire chief," Maggie said, beaming. "It's too bad Colt has already laid claim to you..."

For the zillionth time in the last hour, Brielle felt her cheeks grow warm. And then, to Brielle's absolute horror, the two men began walking their way. She could barely form coherent sentences around Colt, let alone try to hold a conversation with *two* such hunks. Hell, she now lived on a cattle ranch; why not just call them beefcakes?

"Good afternoon, Mom." Hawk leaned down and kissed Maggie on the cheek.

"Hello, son. How did that last call go?" she asked, giving him a quick hug.

Brielle was completely out of her element. The two seemed to have genuine affection for each other. Her family didn't do hugs or kisses anymore. At one time they had, though — a long time ago.

"It was fine. Rick just hit a deer and messed up his truck's bumper. The deer had to be put down, but you know that happens too often," Hawk said.

"I know it does, Hawk, but it's still unpleasant."

Hawk nodded before turning Brielle's way. "Who's this beautiful woman with you, Mom?" he asked with a winning smile.

It was bright enough to make Brielle want to take a step backward. Or forward — she wasn't sure.

"This is Brielle," Colt said, stepping up beside her once again and wrapping his arm back around her. It seemed his fear of the meddling women was overruled by his desire to put his brand on Brielle before Hawk had a chance to get interested.

Not that Brielle realized that.

"Ah...I see," Hawk said with a laugh. "Too bad," he added with a wink at Brielle. "I'm Hawk. If your place is ever on fire, make sure and give me a call."

"Yeah, we'll do that," Colt practically growled.

Hawk laughed with delight. "It was nice having you in the pack for as long as we did, brother."

"I'm still in the pack, Hawk."

"Doesn't look like it to me."

"What pack?" Brielle asked. She was grateful to have found her voice.

Before Colt could stop Hawk from speaking, the man opened his mouth. "The single men's solidarity group," he said with another chuckle. "I'd better grab my jeans and go." He reached out, took Brielle's hand, lifted it to his mouth, and he planted a kiss. "It was a pleasure meeting you, Brielle."

Hawk headed to the counter and grabbed the package that was waiting for him, and then just as quickly as he had come in to the store, he was gone again.

"Yes, too bad," Maggie said with a sigh as she watched the front door close. "I can't wait for him to settle down."

"We really need to pay for our things and get going," Colt said grumpily.

"Of course, sweetie. We wouldn't dream of holding you up," Bethel said as she leaned in and kissed Brielle's cheek. "It was so great to meet you, dear. I'll be sure to have you over for lunch before too long."

The two other women also kissed her, and they repeated the sentiment, then left the store without buying a single thing.

"Did they come over here just to meet me?" Brielle asked.

"Yeah, they did. We'd better get out of here before the entire town comes in," Colt replied, and his tone indicated irritation.

Why was he was in such a foul mood all of a sudden? Brielle had no idea, but it wasn't her place to ask. When they approached the register, Brielle pulled out her bank card — a mere gold card with a laughably low limit — except she wasn't laughing. Yep, the purchase would hurt, but at least she now had boots and could ride a horse. Or could she? She still wasn't going to admit that she'd never done it before.

CHAPTER NINE

THE RIDE BACK to her ranch was filled with tension so thick that Brielle wondered how it was the windows didn't shatter. Colt was in a less than perfect mood, and she thought back to what had happened during their time in the store.

Yes, they'd kissed, and yes, she'd run away from him afterward, but he'd seemed fine while she was speaking with the three surprisingly friendly women. It wasn't until after his friend had arrived that he'd grown so grumpy and distant. Maybe Hawk wasn't really a good friend and Colt didn't like being around him. But she and Colt were hardly the best of friends themselves, so she couldn't ask him about it.

So instead, she just sat there in the passenger seat and hoped for the ride to end as soon as possible. The quicker it was over, the less smothered she'd feel by the claustrophobic air inside his truck. When they finally arrived at the ranch, she bolted.

"Be ready to leave in thirty minutes," Colt yelled after her as she scampered up her front steps.

She didn't bother with a response, because his truck was already pulling away. Not looking back, she went inside the house and looked around critically for the hundredth time as she walked up the staircase toward her bedroom.

No one could call the house luxurious. Its bare walls were begging for a fresh coat of paint. The sparse furnishings that had come with the house were okay for this neck of the woods, she supposed, and some of them were probably considered antiques, but none of it lined up with her typical taste.

She liked modern furniture with clean, crisp edges and bold colors. This ranch house still had red-and-white-checked curtains that looked as if they'd been around since the house was built. The only saving grace was her bedroom.

At least her father had paid to have her furniture shipped in. She'd told him there was no way she was sleeping on some dead person's old mattress. He'd laughed but agreed that he wouldn't do that either.

So, as she stepped into her room, she felt a little cheered up looking at her four-poster bed with teal coverings and whimsical cloth hanging from the corners. The lines of her cherry wood furniture were beautiful, and she loved to sit on the comfortable stool in front of her matching vanity and see her perfumes all in a neat row, each one calling out to be the fragrance du jour.

She turned her shopping bags upside down on the bed and looked at her new purchases. They certainly didn't constitute clothing she ever thought she'd own, but she wanted to see her property on horseback, so she'd do what she had to.

After changing quickly into a pair of snug-fitting Wranglers and a green cotton button-up shirt, she sat down and pulled on the uncomfortable boots. Peggy had assured her that they would form to her feet and that soon she wouldn't want to wear anything else. Yeah, right.

Brielle looked longingly at the heels she'd just taken off. From the time she turned thirteen she'd been wearing them. When a girl was blessed with a height of only five foot three, she needed all the advantages she could get — and they came by wearing the highest heels possible.

Though heels, especially high heels, could cause some major pain after a few hours, it was about the look, the feel of having on a pair of shoes that made you feel taller, prettier, and certainly sexier. She might be in the backwoods of a ranching state, but that didn't mean she needed to throw fashion to the wind. She would never change so much that she didn't care about her appearance. Yes, she could admit that maybe she spent a little too much time on it, but in the world she'd grown up in, looks really did matter.

How sad was that…

Wait. Why was it sad? A woman who could highlight her assets wasn't a rich bimbo; she was just smart. This dang place was sure to ruin her!

Throwing her hair back into a ponytail — wasn't that practical of her? — she decided she'd spent enough time upstairs. If she took too long, she had no doubt, Colt wouldn't wait around for her down at the horse barn. Fighting to get used to the boots as she came down the stairs, Brielle held tight to the railing, keeping her eye on it to make sure no spiders were going to pop out. This would be a much longer drop than the tumble she'd taken off the front porch.

She didn't bother locking her front door after she shut it behind her. It seemed no one here locked doors. As there was very little crime in Sterling, she actually felt safe. It was a weird feeling to go from a world in which the door stayed locked 24/7, to a place where an open door was expected, part of the mind-set.

When she entered the horse barn, she ran smack into Tony, and a little of her excitement vanished. Why did her foreman have to be so grouchy all the time? What was his problem with her? Sure, she didn't want to be in charge of this place, but she did own it, and it would really help if the guy just gave her a chance.

Okay, okay, how much of a chance had she really given him? None, honestly, and she wasn't proud of that. She didn't know anything about him or anything about this ranch. But she was trying to change that, wasn't she? Didn't she get credit for trying? It would sure as heck be nice.

"Colt's over by the arena," Tony grumbled before turning to walk away. Brielle stopped him with a hand on his arm. He looked at her with disapproval but didn't say a word.

"Look, Tony, you know and I know that I don't know *anything* about running a ranch, and I really need your help. Do you think we can come to a truce and maybe work together?"

Brielle was almost surprised by the words coming out of her mouth. It wasn't like her to actually try to compromise. She'd been here only two weeks, and already she was speaking differently, acting differently — as if she'd received the gift of tongues in a foreign land. If this was the big change her father wanted to see, she was going to be ticked, because she didn't want him to be right.

She didn't want to admit that she *needed* to change. Still, she told herself, she needed her foreman if she were to do what she had to do so she could get out of Montana ASAP. That didn't count as changing; it was doing whatever it took to get back to her real life.

Tony looked at her for several moments. Was he trying to see inside her head? His look made her squirm a little — she was surely coming up short in the man's mind. It shouldn't matter to her, but for some reason it really did.

He spit another stream of tobacco. "I will give you a chance when I think you honestly give a damn about this place."

"I do care about it here," she lied.

"That's a joke. Don't for one minute think you can fool an old man. This has been my home since I was in my early teens. I love the land, love the people, love the animals even more. Some little city girl doesn't get to come in with all her daddy's money and act like my home ain't good enough for her. I don't appreciate that none." Surprisingly, his voice stayed level throughout.

"I am *not* some spoiled little brat," she told him. "And if you care so much about this place, why is it failing?"

"Maybe that's something you'll have to find out. Anyway, from the talk I had with your daddy, he realizes he made some mistakes along the way. I don't believe you can do this at all, *Miss* Storm."

Her fists clenched at her sides. "That's the rudest thing I've ever heard."

"I wasn't trying to be rude, just stating the facts," Tony said before turning away to leave.

"I wasn't done speaking to you," she said, frustration clear in her tone, making him pause before turning back toward her.

"When I feel you have something valuable to say, I'll chat longer." And with that, he walked away, leaving Brielle stunned, hurt, and extremely pissed off.

"I should fire him right now," she muttered, but then clasped a hand over her mouth. She really didn't want him to overhear that. She wasn't so naïve as to think this place could run without him. And one way or another she'd get Tony to like her, although after those words of his, she shouldn't give a damn what he thought about her.

No, wouldn't happen. That man would always do what he wanted. Even if he *loved* her — sure, sure — he would still do things his own way. That was just the sort of man he was. Stubborn. Ornery. Set in his ways.

Brielle found her temper waning as she made her way to the arena. She was shocked when she realized that she sort of liked the gruff old guy. And she should have hated him on principle alone.

When she turned a corner and looked up, she found Colt putting a saddle on a majestic brown horse that she was sure she should know the breed of, but she knew less than nothing about horses. The horse, unfortunately, wasn't the only majestic creature in the place. The way Colt's muscles bulged made her slightly lightheaded. This man was much finer than the guys she normally hung out with, despite their expensively honed gym bodies. Yeah, working on a ranch seemed to do good things to a lot of the population of Sterling. At least from what she'd seen so far.

"You've ridden before, right?"

Brielle was startled to realize Colt was speaking to her. No, she hadn't ridden, not even once.

"Of course I have."

Sauntering over to the horse, she thought back to the cowboy movies she'd watched, put her foot into the stirrup and hefted herself onto his back. She was a little wobbly, but felt immense pride as she sat astride this massive animal. And she was facing the right way.

Man, it was a long way to the ground.

"I picked Bluegrass because she's pretty mellow. I figured the only horses you've ridden have been at some hoity-toity country club."

She? Oops. She should have inspected the horse more closely. "Well, you can figure what you want. I don't care," she said, hating that everyone's opinion of her was so poor.

This man was going to drive her nuts — he was presumptuous and ill-mannered. If she could go riding with anyone else, she'd be much better off, but so far there were no other volunteers.

"This ride will take a while, Ms. Storm, so hold on and follow my lead." Colt walked over to an even bigger horse than hers, one who was pure black and seemed jittery as he — or she? — waited to be ridden. She really should ask what breed the horses were, but if she did, he'd probably look at her with that maddening gleam in his eyes that screamed "city girl."

As she wobbled in her saddle, Brielle started thinking that maybe she'd made a mistake, but then as they started out from the barn, the only thing she could concentrate on was trying not to fall off. She didn't have any more time to worry about what would happen if she couldn't manage to hold on.

CHAPTER TEN

WHEN THE OPEN grass on the hills did nothing for him, Colt knew he was in a seriously bad mood. It was foolish, really — no, it was completely ridiculous — but watching Hawk flirt with Brielle had thoroughly pissed him off.

Yes, Colt knew logically that it had been harmless, and yes, he knew Hawk was even more afraid of commitment than he was, but still, he couldn't banish the jealousy. Hawk had been his friend since the first day of kindergarten, but that didn't mean they hadn't always enjoyed competing with each other.

Actually, an entire group of them really liked to push each other to the limits, to see how far they could take things. It was good for them and never before had jealousy been an issue.

Never before today.

Colt had practically seen red when he witnessed Brielle's reaction to meeting Hawk. But at least he had his answer on whether to sleep with this woman.

If he didn't, he had a feeling she wouldn't leave his consciousness alone. And she was something that he couldn't have haunting him for the rest of his days. He didn't want to be in a "relationship" with her. She was a city girl, a spoiled little princess.

But there was just something about her, something that was calling to him. She was on his mind all the time, and he didn't understand why or how.

Yes, he'd been seriously attracted to women before, but the second they left his sight, they also vanished from this thoughts. Women served a purpose, a very important purpose, but still just a purpose. A means to an end. And she had a cute little end...

Anyway, once his needs were met, Colt was fine with walking away, and then finding the next woman when his desires began to cloud his judgment again. If it looked as if a woman wasn't interested, which happened just about never, he would move happily on to the next.

If he wasn't sexually attracted to them, once in a blue moon they'd become a friend, but most of the time he just wouldn't strike up a conversation. Whichever way it went, it didn't affect him, didn't leave him with longing, didn't leave him in such a disagreeable mood.

After about ten minutes of riding out along the borders of Brielle's property, he decided he'd better get the air cleared up. He was supposed to be showing her the land, and he certainly couldn't point things out if he wasn't speaking to the silly woman. He had to hand it to her, though — she knew when to be silent.

That was a quality he could appreciate in a woman. ... Damn. If his mama had ever heard him say such a crude thing, of course, she'd have smacked him in the back of the head. He almost flinched just thinking about it.

Yeah, Colt knew he could be an ass, but weren't all men at some point? *Yeah, they were*, he assured himself. Even if he knew he was full of bullshit, along with that whole *boys will be boys* mentality.

"It looked like you and Hawk were getting quite cozy back there at the store." *Dammit.* Colt wanted to kick himself for his words and the tone in which he'd delivered them, but it was now out in the open and he couldn't take the statement back, so he might as well hold his ground.

When Brielle whipped her head around, and her horse took a side step, most likely from the tension in the woman's legs, Colt didn't know what to think. Was she upset that she'd been caught drooling over his friend, or was she pissed at what he'd just said?

"What in the hell is that supposed to mean?"

"Well, it didn't take you long to forget that we'd been making out in the changing room right before Hawk walked into the place." Again, he wished he could take the words back, but his brain seemed to be sending him messages just a few seconds too late.

"You know what, Colt?"

He waited but she didn't say anything. "What?" he finally asked.

"You're a complete jerk! I don't know why I thought it would be good to have you show me the grounds. If you think I'm such a slut, then why in the hell did you kiss me at all?" she snapped. "Oh, I get it! It was *because* you think I'm a slut that you were enjoying the make-out session. Do you think I should just climb off this horse right now and climb on top of you? After all, that's what whores do, right? They can go to town with one guy and then climb aboard the next one as soon as they're finished."

Her fury had the odd effect of calming him. Granted, he'd just made a fool of himself. But if she'd been attracted to Hawk, why would she be so outraged now? She wouldn't. She'd blush, or turn her head, or giggle or something, wouldn't she?

Hell, Colt didn't know. It wasn't as if he had a lot of experience with this sort of thing. Normally, if a girl liked one of his friends more than she liked him, he was fine to see her go off into the night with the guy.

This was the first time in his life that he wanted to fight for the girl, and that made zero sense to him. Brielle was just a city girl, a girl who wouldn't be here very long, a girl who was forgettable. Wasn't she?

Somehow, he knew that wasn't the case. Though she was all wrong for him, he had a feeling he wouldn't be able to wash this girl right out of his hair so easily. He had a feeling that if he didn't move fast, he'd lose her before he ever had the chance to have her.

That thought filled him with dread, which meant that he should be running as fast as he could in the opposite direction. Instead, he found himself trying to make up with her.

"I'm sorry. That was rude. It's just that I felt…" He didn't know how to end that sentence, and found himself falling silent.

"You felt like an ass? Like a tyrant? Like a slimeball?"

"Yeah, a little bit like all of those things," he said, and then his lips turned up and soon he was hitting her with his best smile. The widening of her eyes told him that she wasn't unaffected by him.

"Good," she said, then jerked her head away and concentrated on her riding.

"How about we call a truce? You forget that I've been an ass, and I'll…" She hadn't done anything wrong, so how could he complete that sentence?

"And I'll…?" she asked.

"Just sit there, beautiful, and let me tell you about the land." When her cheeks filled with color, he figured he'd finally done something right. Though she must have been told she was beautiful all the time, maybe it was by people who wanted something from her, so it didn't mean as much.

That thought sent a bolt to his stomach. He also wanted something from her — her land. She just didn't realize that yet. He was such a freaking fool to think he could begin something with this woman. There was no possible way it could ever lead to anything but disaster, because when she found out that he didn't really work for her — that, in fact, he was deceiving her with a rather crass ulterior motive — she'd never speak to him again.

Wasn't that ideal, though? He could have fun with her now, give them both a lot of pleasure, and then walk away guilt free. Of course, how was he going to walk away without guilt when he already felt terrible about what he was doing?

Thrusting that thought away, he decided just to enjoy the moment.

"You know already that you have ten thousand acres. There are usually a couple of hundred head of cattle on the south side of the property, but not this year, because of finances. And the north side is where your fields are. You grow soft white wheat, which will be ready to harvest about the end of July or beginning of August. The ranches around here have seen some hard times lately and a lot of them are losing money, but your father is convinced this land is rich and you can turn it around."

Colt paused. He was sure the land could be turned around, too, but did he really want to tell her that? If he was supposed to be trying to persuade her to leave, he didn't want to tell her how valuable her land was, did he?

Of course, he wouldn't be playing fair then, and he didn't believe in lies, didn't believe in beating an opponent without giving him — okay, her — all the facts. It made victory less satisfying.

"Do *you* think it can be saved?"

She was looking at him trustingly, and Colt knew he couldn't lie to her. No way.

"Yes. I think this ranch can do a lot better than it has. Tony is an excellent foreman and he does the best job he can with the budget he's been given, but the previous owners were swimming in debt, and they had too much pride to ask for help. By the time I knew what was going on, Donald had passed away and his wife was in mourning."

"What could you have done?"

Colt winced when she asked that question. This was the reason lying was never good — you always had to be so careful with what you said. There had been plenty he could have done, and first and foremost was to buy the property. He'd never know why they hadn't just sold it to him.

He would have let them stay in the house until they were gone and he would have taken care of their land. *Foolish pride* was all he could think.

The couple hadn't had children to pass the land down to, and it would have worked out so much better for all of them. But why waste time wondering? He would never have the answer. And he was dealing with Brielle now. That's what he needed to remember.

"We all help each other out here," he said, hoping that would be good enough for her.

When she didn't question him further, he breathed out a sigh of relief. Brielle was apparently a lot more trusting than he was.

"You have really rich soils, superb pastureland, and a year-round supply of fresh water running through your land from a mountain spring." Water from that same spring also ran through his land, but he left that part out.

When the two of them approached some low tree limbs over the trail, Colt ducked easily and didn't think anything of it until he heard Brielle cry out. After turning in his saddle to look, he whipped his horse around, then jumped off.

Brielle was lying on the ground with a grimace of pain on her face.

"What happened?" Colt knelt down next to her and looked around for signs of a snake that might have startled her horse, or for any other reason she'd been thrown.

"I don't know," she said while trying to sit up and then wincing. That's when he noticed the rip on her jeans, and some blood on her hip. She'd landed on a jagged rock. Bending down, he examined the cut.

"It doesn't look too deep, but we need to get antiseptic on it to prevent infection. It will hurt for a few days, but other than that, it should heal fine. Let me grab some things to help clean and wrap it." He got up, went to his saddlebag, and pulled out some first-aid supplies.

His horse was trained so well that he didn't have to tie him to a tree. Shadow would stay until Colt told him to go and graze. They were so in tune with each other that the horse knew when Colt needed to ride fast and release energy or go slow and examine the land. Even the slightest of movements from Colt let his horse know what he wanted.

Returning to Brielle, Colt became suspicious when he glanced over at Bluegrass. The mare was calm and munching away on some nearby grass. The animal hadn't been spooked, so it seemed as if Brielle had simply fallen off. Why?

"Were you telling me the truth earlier? Have you ridden before?"

When her cheeks flushed and she refused to meet his gaze, Colt was furious. "You don't lie about something like that, Brielle. You could have been seriously injured, far worse than the few bumps you have right now. This land isn't smooth and it's not a trail for beginners."

"I wanted to ride, to see the land, and you never would have brought me out here if you'd known I hadn't been on a horse before," she said, her shoulders tense, her eyes determined.

He had to respect her for wanting to learn more about the area, but he didn't appreciate being lied to, especially about something so important.

"I still would have brought you out," he said, though she was probably right — he most likely wouldn't have, certainly not while she was astride her own horse.

"No, you wouldn't have. Everyone here pretends I don't even exist. I'm sick of it! I own this place and no one will let me do anything!"

Colt's anger diminished as her voice rose. Did she actually want to learn how to run this place, or was she just frustrated because she didn't know how? He was confused, and it was an emotion he wasn't used to.

So instead of facing the issue, he focused on bandaging her up. He had to think. That's the only thing that would help right now. They were about an hour away from the house now, or maybe a little more, depending on how slowly they went. And they'd gotten such a late start.

He was quiet as he finished up, and then he looked at her and took a deep breath. "You're going to have to ride on my horse on the way back."

He knew that was going to test every ounce of endurance and control he had in his body. Because now wasn't the time to see how much chemistry the two of them had together.

She gaped at him, and took in a few of her own deep breaths. "I'll be fine on my own horse."

"Sorry, Princess. You ride with me, or we both walk, and I'm telling you, we're a long way from the house if we go by foot."

He was firm, and her eyes narrowed. He knew she hated it when he called her Princess, and she also hated to be told what to do, but it was something she was going to have to get used to. She deserved that name. Besides, he had to create distance between the two of them if he was expected to ride with her pressed against him for the next hour.

"Whatever, Colt," she said at last, though her body was tense as he helped her to her feet. She was limping when he led her over to his horse, and he knew she was in more pain than she was letting on. This wasn't going to be a pleasant ride for either of them.

The sun was getting low in the sky, and they'd be lucky to make it back to the house before it set. Gathering the reins to her horse, he tied a lead rope on, and then helped Brielle up on his horse before joining her and setting out toward her house with Brielle sitting in front of him — with her curvy ass pressed against him.

This was going to test him to the very limits. They were silent as they rode the miles back to her place, and Colt recited every church hymn he could remember. It was a good thing his mother had made him attend Sunday school for so many years. Maybe it was time to start going again.

Conversation. They needed to have a conversation.

"Where did you grow up?"

Brielle was quiet for so long that he thought she was just going to ignore him. When he'd given up, she finally spoke. "In Maine. It was a small seaside town, but I loved it as a kid."

"And did that change?" he asked when she paused a while.

"Everything changes," she said with such a sigh that he felt it run through him. What was her real story? When she was silent for a while longer, he decided to speak about himself.

"I grew up right here in Sterling. Loved it then, love it now. This community, while very small, has the greatest people you will ever want to know. I could go anywhere, but I choose to stay here."

"Have you ever left?"

In the moment, Colt didn't even think about the fact that he was supposed to be a ranch hand. "Yeah, I've done some traveling. I got my MBA at Harvard. Met some of my best friends there. To this day we're still as close as brothers."

"Harvard? You went to Harvard and you're a ranch hand?"

Crap! There was the thing about lying again. He was silent for a minute while he tried how to answer as honestly as he could.

"I had amazing parents, the best in the world. They died five years ago while on vacation in Oregon. Black ice. I was devastated. But I worked hard in school, got excellent grades, and played basketball." That was honest, at least.

"Wow. That's impressive, Colt. But why ranch if you have an MBA from Harvard? You could go anywhere with that, make so much money."

"I grew up here, and I love it here. I knew when I went to college that I would come back home." That was also true. She just didn't know he was extremely wealthy. She didn't need to know that right now. Maybe never. Well, that wasn't true. She would have to know when he bought her land.

"I went to Brown," she admitted shyly.

"You're pretty impressive yourself, Brielle." Colt didn't add that he was surprised to hear it.

"I don't tell too many people, because I didn't finish. I had one year left, English major. I once thought I would write for the *New York Times*, or *USA Today*, and then I thought maybe *Time* magazine. Then, that dwindled to a fashion magazine; then it all just sort of fell away." Her voice trailed off in embarrassment.

"Why? Why would you quit if that's your passion?"

"Probably similar reasons to yours, though not as noble. I had a bad experience at the end of my junior year of college and I wanted to go home. I hadn't planned on returning home, but after that, I tucked in my tail and ran, and home is where I landed. My relationship with my father and brothers was already shot by that point, but I still knew I could come back; I still knew it was a safe zone."

"Was it a guy?"

"No, nothing that typical," she said with a laugh that he was glad to hear. "I had a professor I didn't get along with, and a roommate who betrayed me. Really, I think back, and I know it was stupid to leave. I know I should have just moved out of that apartment, and transferred out of the professor's class, but I was spoiled and frustrated, and..." She trailed off as she thought about past decisions.

"I think all of us make choices in life that we wish we could take back. Those choices don't define us, though, Brielle. If we learn from them, we grow."

She was silent for a while after his words, either processing them or rejecting them. Colt wished he could see her face, read her expression.

"Well, I landed here. I don't know how wisely my choices have been to let that happen." She added a laugh as if it were a joke, but he could hear the pain in her voice. She really thought very little of herself. It didn't help that he had judged her quickly and harshly.

But what had he been supposed to think? First impressions mattered, and their first encounter hadn't gone well. Colt was now more confused than ever before because he was beginning to find out more about this woman, and it wasn't all bad — some was pretty damn good.

She was intelligent, but she seemed to hide behind a mask of vanity. One thing he knew for sure about Brielle Storm was that he had no idea what tomorrow would bring.

They got lost in their own heads for the last twenty minutes of their ride to the ranch, and just as he'd suspected, the sun was almost all the way down by the time they reached her horse barn.

He was beginning to get on edge as he tried to figure out his jumbled thoughts about this complicated woman, so when the next words from her mouth were a complaint, he didn't react well.

"How does anyone ride horses day and night?"

"You get used to it."

"I can get down myself," she snapped when he held out a hand to assist her from the horse.

"I know you can. I was just trying to be helpful."

Colt had to admit he was surprised when she gripped the harness and hoisted herself off the horse, her legs shaking but somehow still managing to hold her up. Well, the day wasn't quite over yet, as she was about to find out.

"How is your hip feeling?" She was limping slightly, but not too badly. She'd live.

"I'm fine," she told him with enough heat that he knew she was indeed fine. *So fine.*

"Good. We need to brush down the horses, then."

Brielle looked at him as if he were sprouting horns. "No. I'm going inside now."

Colt lost his smile. "They've worked hard for us. We need to give them a brushing." His voice was firm, but she'd asked to be taught and this was a valuable lesson. Even if they were exhausted, their horses still needed to be taken care of.

"Well, have at it," she told him as she turned to leave.

"I won't take you out again if you don't take care of your animal," he said.

"You work for me, Colt. Don't forget that." She then turned again.

"Don't get too overconfident, Brielle. It makes you look like a spoiled little snot, and that happens way too often." He wasn't even attempting to be pleasant now. Though there'd been a nice stretch in the middle, the day had gone rather badly and was aiming to end even worse.

She turned to glare while still walking away, and that's when her foot sank into in a big pile of fresh horse dung.

"That's it!" she yelled, causing several heads to turn in her direction. "Look all you want! I've had it with this stinky, smelly place."

The men in there were trying desperately to quiet their laughter, but after she was gone and the echo of her front door being slammed could be heard all the way down in the horse barn, the men let go and laughed aloud.

"That's enough," Colt warned them, and they stopped at once. "She may be having a difficult time here, but she does own the place. You might want to remember that."

"Aw, Colt. You'll own it soon enough," one of the hands said.

"I don't know, Brandon. She may be a pain in the ass, but I think a lot of it's an act. That woman has more backbone than I would have given her credit for on the first day I met her," Colt told the young man.

None of the men knew how to respond to that, so they shut up. They were so sure the city girl would run off into the night that they hadn't even considered the possibility that she might actually stick around.

Colt decided it was a good time to head home. He handed Brielle's horse over to Brandon to take care of, then climbed on board his stallion, and rode off.

One thing was certain. He had a lot to think about.

CHAPTER ELEVEN

FOR TWO DAYS Brielle refused to leave her house. It was probably the only place in the entire county where the door was locked and the lights were off. She didn't want to see anyone, and didn't want to climb from her bed. She was embarrassed that she'd opened up to Colt, and more embarrassed about her snotty attitude afterward.

But that's what Brielle did. When she was afraid, when she began to let someone in, she had to fix it quickly, keep that person away. Because if she let them in to her heart, they had power to break it.

That had happened once when she was thirteen, a naïve idiot full of absurd hopes. It wouldn't happen again. Shaking her head, she shut down her memories of that horrible day so long ago. She'd told herself she wouldn't think about it, and she wasn't going to. No way.

She'd made her way downstairs a few times and fetched food to carry back to her room and eat in bed, but other than that, she stayed upstairs and popped Advil like candy to relieve her miserable muscles and the ache in her hip where the deep scratch burned.

A few hot baths, a lot of movies, and about sixty hours were just what she needed, though. Because on the third day, she woke up to find she wasn't hurting nearly as badly.

She could run this ranch without looking like a spoiled brat. The key was to not open up to anyone, to keep it all about business. If she did that, she'd be tough, ready for anything. Brielle knew she was smart, even if most people didn't see that. She chose for them not to. Just one more effective barrier against the world.

Falling from the horse, then stepping in the horse manure, aching so badly she thought she was going to die, and hearing the men laugh at her had all added up to her finding herself at the breaking point. But she wasn't going to prove all of them right and be the pampered princess they were making her out to be.

If she wanted to work, she could. That was for sure. So what was she going to do about it? That was the real question. As she took a nice long hot shower, the wheels in her brain were turning. What had she done in the past when things hadn't gone her way?

She found a solution, that's what she did. So how did she get the young ranch hands to listen to her? There was nothing she could do if they weren't willing to follow her lead. Of course, that was sort of like the blind leading the blind, but, dammit, she was the leader whether they liked it or not.

She didn't want to take advantage of them; she just wanted them to help her make this place a success so her father wouldn't think she was a failure. Somewhere in the past couple of weeks, his opinion had begun to matter to her. Not that she would ever tell him.

Somewhere along the way she had switched her thinking. Maybe it was her conversation with Colt, though she wished that hadn't happened. And maybe it was just that she'd had so much time on her own. Maybe it was even the ranching books she'd been flipping through, and all the Web pages. But, whatever the reason, she had made a decision to do this, and so she would. But she knew she couldn't do it without serious help.

Yes, she still wanted to get away from Montana, but before now, she'd wanted to get away at any cost. Now, it was more important for her to walk away with her head held high.

If she made the place a success and then sold it, her father would be proud, and she'd show her brothers that she wasn't some stupid little girl — that she was just as capable as, or even more capable than, any of them. It's not as if any of those boys had been prizes in the past.

So she needed to figure out how to get the men to listen to her. Once she had their attention, she could work on the respect part. A smile split her face when she figured it out. They were *men*, after all!

Got it! First get them to see her, and then she could make them listen!

*****

Colt had no idea why he was working like a flipping ranch hand on Brielle's property when he had his own land to deal with, but here he was speaking with Tony after helping the men mend fences for the last two hours. It was insane. For her to think he worked for her was one thing, but now he found himself *actually* working for her, and for nothing.

What in the world was wrong with him? His eyes wandered toward the house for the hundredth time in the past ten minutes. He hadn't seen her since she'd stomped off after their ride, and for the first day afterward he was glad of it — or he'd told himself he was.

She'd acted like an overprivileged twit, but that was just the thing — it was an *act*. He knew that. She had been feeling vulnerable, she'd been tired, sore, and hurting. So instead of admitting this, she'd stormed off, making them think the worst of her. What he wanted to know was why?

Still, with her obvious dislike for the land and her obvious incompetence, he'd sworn to himself that first day after their ride that he was going to try to convince her that ranching wasn't the life for her. That shouldn't be too hard. She hated Montana and hated everything to do with the land she now owned. If he could just find the right buttons to push, he'd be all set at getting her to run far, far away.

And yet the thought of her leaving didn't make him ecstatic; instead, it brought him an ache he couldn't quite explain. There was no chance he was falling for this woman. Impossible. Not after a few encounters, a couple of hot kisses, and one "meaningful" conversation.

But he had a sinking feeling about this whole mess — he was certainly falling in lust with the little princess. And that was almost as bad in his book. She was beginning to fill his dreams, and then she was the first thought on his mind when he awoke. He had to get her out of his mind, and he'd already established the only way to do it — have sex with her.

He *had* to do it! For the sake of his sanity. Who could get hurt when it all — or the two of them — came down to it?

A few minutes later, his eyes were rooted to her house when the front door opened. Without realizing it, he was holding his breath. Two and a half days had been too long. That should have stopped him cold, but when she emerged, all thoughts and feelings he had went straight to his lower regions, and he knew he was in deep manure.

The men on lunch break instantly became tongue-tied. Not that he noticed. All his attention was focused on Brielle and what she was wearing — or, more accurately, what she wasn't wearing.

Standing there on the porch and holding a pitcher that looked to be full of lemonade, she had on cutoff jeans — those Wranglers she'd killed on the trail? — that were so damn tiny that the pockets were sticking out of the front. He couldn't imagine what would be showing in the back. And the only thing covering her breasts was about the tiniest bikini top he'd ever seen. What in the hell was she trying to do to him? As he looked around, he revised his question. What was she trying to do to all of them?

"What's going on here?" This came from Tony, who was at his side, and who seemed just as entranced by the show as the rest of the men.

"I don't know, but I'm about to find out," Colt growled.

"Hold on. I want to see what's on her mind," Tony said with a scowl wrinkling his forehead.

"Why? She should know better than to dress like that in front of all these young pups," Colt snapped.

"They've seen less in the way of clothing," Tony said with a chuckle. It was amazing. Even though what sounded like a laugh escaped his mouth, his lips still didn't turn up. Colt would someday have to ask him how he managed that.

Against his better judgment, Colt listened to Tony and decided to see how this was going to play out. When she stepped off the porch and walked to the back of her truck, setting a tray down that held lemonade, what appeared to be cookies, and a lot of paper cups, he began to figure it out.

When she turned, she didn't even look his way, just grabbed the attention of a few of the guys who weren't far away. "Are you boys thirsty?" she asked, her voice dripping honey.

The responses weren't anywhere close to coherent as the men raced toward her and all but salivated at her feet as she poured a cup for each of them. Within the next ten minutes, more than twenty of her employees showed up. Text messages must have been flying. And she was soon surrounded as she sat on the back of the truck, her legs swinging, and her rapt audience hanging on every word she said.

"I've had just about enough of this," Colt said.

"Yeah, but I want to know the point of all this. Come on, humor an old man and give it just a few more minutes," Tony told him.

Colt felt like punching something, but instead, as the two men spoke, he leaned against the side of a tractor, letting the big piece of equipment shade him. He kept his hat pulled low over his eyes as his gaze bored into Brielle.

"Do you know where the hose is? I want to wash my truck." The sound of her sweet voice easily drifted over to him, and his eyes narrowed. He'd bet every dollar he had — and he had plenty — that Brielle had never in her life washed her own vehicle.

So why was she so keen on taking care of a truck that he hadn't seen her drive once since she'd pulled up on her first day at the ranch? When one of the boys fetched her the hose, while another got her a bucket and soap, he waited, now just as curious as Tony.

When the water started and she sprayed the hose high in the air so it cascaded down on her and all the men surrounding her, the sound of her laugher floating happily through the air, he had his answer.

The boys were now looking at her as if she were their golden idol, and he had no doubt in his mind that this was preplanned. She'd figured out how to get the men on her side, and she'd done it with both guns blazing.

He almost wanted to clap his hands and congratulate her. She wasn't as defeated as he'd thought she was. When she lifted the sudsy sponge from the bucket and began washing the side of the truck, her hips swaying, drawing every pair of eyes to her rich assets, he was finished. She could play all the games she wanted to play, but what she was about to learn was that if she wanted to play with fire, she was damn well going to get burned.

No longer aware of Tony's presence, Colt pushed off from the side of the tractor and approached Brielle and her posse of men. He was only a few feet away when she turned and noticed him, the hose in her hand forgotten, the spout pointing directly at him.

The cool shot of water to his chest didn't faze him. It was refreshing, actually, since he was hot as hell. Without a word, but with the water still spraying him and soaking his jeans, Colt began unbuttoning his shirt.

"Oh...sorry," she said, as if just realizing what was happening.

He didn't care. She set down the hose and acted as if she were going to turn away, but his eyes held hers, and he wasn't giving her permission to break the connection.

He peeled his shirt from his wet shoulders, and felt immense pleasure when her eyes widened and she took her time looking at his rock-hard upper body. Yeah, she'd seen it before, but he couldn't help but feel good that she was obviously mesmerized. That wouldn't hurt for what was coming next.

"Leave." Though his gaze never left hers, the young men around her had no doubt that he was speaking to them. They scattered faster than a group of horses with a pit of snakes thrown into their corral.

With a look of triumph, Colt began moving toward his prey. He didn't know when or how, but somewhere, somehow, Brielle had become his, and it was now time he proved it to her.

CHAPTER TWELVE

THOUGH BRIELLE HAD never received a look like the one Colt was sending her way now, she had no problem figuring out exactly what it meant. He wanted her, and he was coming after what he wanted. She was frozen where she stood, unable to tear her eyes from his. She absolutely didn't want this feeling buzzing all through her body to go away.

She had come out to win the men over, and she'd been more than successful — they were practically eating out of her hand right now. But she hadn't expected the reaction she was getting from Colt. Sure, she knew he wanted her. Hadn't that been obvious from the kisses they'd shared? But the hunger burning in his eyes was beyond what she'd ever seen before.

Was she afraid? She couldn't answer that.

His look was sending her body into overdrive and she was more than willing to answer the animal lust in his expression. Her mind was doing its best to tell her this was wrong, was trying to stop her from making a mistake.

Its best wasn't anywhere in the vicinity of good enough. When he stopped right in front of her, she didn't care what her brain was saying.

All she cared about was how her body felt, and as he placed his hand on the back of her neck, she knew she wasn't going to tell him no.

The only thing she was going to do was faint if he didn't lean down and kiss her right this second. As if he could read her mind, he lowered his head, and then fireworks exploded when his lips captured her.

This time, he wasn't slow. This time, he didn't ask silently by softly touching his tongue to her lips. No. This time, he was showing her that he was in charge. He was pressing his body against hers and it was already hard and ready and sending all the right signals to her core. His tongue demanded entrance into her mouth, and she was ready for him, too.

Melting against the slick hardness of Colt's chest, and with his strong arms caging her in, Brielle surrendered happily. She wrapped her arms around his solid shoulders and held on tight while he kissed her more deeply than any other man had ever come close.

When his hand slipped down her nearly naked back and clutched the wet material of her short shorts, she moaned into his mouth, forgetting there was anyone else on the ranch. She ached for his touch, ached for him to quench the flames blazing through her.

When he pulled back, she whimpered, not understanding why he would possibly stop when they were just beginning. "House, now!" was his answer to her unspoken question, and then the breath was pushed from her lungs when he lifted her up and hoisted her over his shoulder.

Brielle was horrified. He was carrying her caveman style into the house, and in front of who knew how many of her workers, but when he slammed the door shut behind them, and she opened her mouth to protest his Neanderthal ways, he simply pressed her against the door and began where he'd left off back at her truck.

Any and all objections faded away.

She was lost as he gripped her thighs and lifted her, letting the door help hold her up as his body pressed against hers and he pushed against her core, making the fire burning deep inside turn her into red-hot lava.

His mouth commandeered hers as he traced her lips with his sure tongue before entering again and making her veins tingle and throb. He cupped her sweetly rounded behind with his hand as she clamped her legs tightly around him.

When he slipped his fingers beneath the hem of her cutoffs and touched her flesh, she moaned, opening her mouth further to his probing tongue.

This wasn't what she'd planned when she started out of the house late this morning, but as he pushed against her, she understood that plans were made to be broken. *Best-laid* plans. This was a much better way to spend her afternoon.

"I need you, Brielle," he groaned, after barely pulling back far enough from her mouth to speak.

"Then take me, Colt." She let her head fall back against the door, and he began nibbling down her neck.

"Please tell me you're sure..."

Why did he need to say this? She didn't want to think about whether or not she was sure, didn't want to analyze the situation. All she wanted to do right now was feel — feel everything he was doing to her, and more.

"Yes," she said, because she was sure that if they didn't complete this, she would curl up and die.

That settled that. Still holding her against him, he pushed away from the door and began moving to the staircase. She didn't ask him how he knew where her room was; she was too focused on the way he was licking along her neck.

He climbed the stairs with her in his arms, and he didn't even grow short of breath. That was something for her to think about later. The sheer strength this man possessed was a huge turn-on for her. She'd never been carried off before. And she'd never felt so sure of anything in her life.

When he reached her room, she was ready for him to rip her clothes right off, but he somehow managed to set her down gently on the bed, then step back and take a long look at the picture she made.

Her flesh was pink, her nipples hard, and her shorts too tight. She wanted all barriers between them gone. As if reading her mind, he reached down and began undoing his jeans. She couldn't remove her gaze from the beautiful trail of hair that led to the buttons there. Each one that he undid brought her that much closer to seeing his magnificence.

At last, he grabbed his jeans and briefs in tight fingers and pushed them down. She gaped helplessly at his lean hips, the ripples in his abs, and each glorious inch of flesh below that he displayed for her greedy eyes.

Because the denim was wet, it took a little more effort for him to peel his jeans away, but it was worth the wait, because when he freed himself, she gasped in delight.

"Oh, Colt, I'm so ready for this," she sighed, practically drooling as his manhood sprung forth in all its breathtaking glory. He was thick, solid, and more than primed for combat, and the sheen on the head of all that flesh made her bite her lip in anticipation.

He had to groan, and, hearing that, she lifted her eyes upward to meet his, which were burning with desire. "If you keep looking at me like I'm the main course, I won't last long enough for either of us to fully enjoy this," he warned her as he joined her on the bed.

"Colt, you're not the main course — you are most certainly the best course: dessert," she replied with a come-hither smile.

And he came hither. With another growl, he lay on top of her and captured her lips once more, ravishing her mouth before turning both their bodies sideways so he could pull the string at the back of her bikini top.

In two seconds flat her breasts were freed and she reveled in the feel of them pressing against his muscled chest. She wriggled to get even closer.

No dice. He pushed her on her back and trailed his mouth down her neck, licking the skin before nipping it and making her cry out for more. Moving farther down her body, he circled his mouth around each of her luscious breasts in turn, teasing her, taking his time to get to the hard peaks she so desperately wanted him to suck.

"Now, Colt. Please." She lifted her hands into his hair and guided him there. And he was finally fastening on one sensitive bud and taking the pink flesh into his mouth while swiping his tongue across its aching surface.

She cried out as she felt the heat building inside her, felt herself on the edge of exploding, and he hadn't even touched her core yet. If loving this was wrong, she didn't want to be right.

He moved to her other breast and gave it ample attention before running his tongue down the center of her cleavage and making his way to her stomach, sucking and licking every inch of quivering flesh.

When he undid her cutoffs and began stripping them away, she lifted her hips from the bed to make it easier for him, needing his mouth where she was pulsing with hunger. He didn't make her wait long.

After getting rid of her tiny shorts and tinier panties, he spread her legs and licked her inner thighs, growling in his appreciation of her hot scent before he moved upward and ran his tongue along her sensitive folds.

When he clamped his lips onto the pulsing bud of her womanhood, she jerked up from the bed, and the greatest pleasure of all ripped through her in wave after blissful wave.

"Yes," she cried out, clasping her hands in his hair and holding him there, afraid he would stop before she was ready for him to.

She had nothing to fear on that score. He swept his tongue across her flesh in time with the pulsations of her body, and drew out her pleasure for so long that when it ended, she collapsed against the mattress.

She was spent. There was no possible way she could do more, and it was just too bad for him. As if he could read her mind, he chuckled. "Don't get too comfortable, Brielle. We aren't finished," he told her, and he slipped two fingers inside her hot sheath.

"Oh, Colt, I can't..." she started to say, but the words ended on a moan, because somehow he was hitting just the right spot to make her body come alive again.

He moved his fingers slowly in and out, building the embers of her fire to a red-hot blaze once again, and she was soon writhing beneath him. His fingers just weren't enough.

"Colt..."

"Tell me what you want, Brielle."

He was going to make her say it, and sadly, she didn't have an ounce of shame as she replied: "You. Inside me. Right now."

He pulled his fingers from her and then climbed up her body, leaving a trail of kisses all the way to her lips. She tried to turn away, the thought of tasting herself on his tongue making her uneasy, but he gripped her head and plunged inside her mouth, giving her a new sensation as his musky flavor mixed with hers. Not bad, really — she could definitely get used to that. And as the head of his arousal pressed to her core, she opened her legs wider, needing him to thrust inside, forgetting about anything but the two of them making the ultimate connection.

As his tongue grazed her lips, he slipped an inch of his erection inside her, making her tremble with wanting. "Please," she begged again as she wrapped her legs around him. The anticipation was killing her. She wanted to feel his thickness inside her. She wanted completion.

Then he thrust his tongue inside her mouth at the same time as he drove inside her body, swallowing the scream she released. So full, so possessed. She felt perfect right now, or so she thought.

When he began moving, slowly at first, in and out, and then picking up speed and building her to a fiery peak, she knew this was as good as it could possibly get. Never before had she been so over the edge in passion that the world faded away, but that's exactly what was happening now as Colt held her willing body.

She could do this forever, and still it wouldn't be enough. They moved in perfect rhythm as he took her to the very best place she could ever be, and when they came together in a brilliant flash of light and heat, her body shook with the power of the release.

Colt's groans echoed through the room, music to her ears. The weight of his now relaxed body was a perfect blanket, and in this moment she was in total and utter peace.

CHAPTER THIRTEEN

BRIELLE FELT AS if she were drifting on a raft in a peaceful lake as Colt held her securely against his chest and his fingers traced shapes in her back. The sensation was beyond compare, and if she could freeze this moment, she would be the happiest woman alive.

Okay, maybe not. Reality would soon set in, but for now, her body was sated, her heart was full, and she felt as if she didn't have a single worry.

"Why do you put on an act, Brielle?"

His tone was soft, gentle, not accusing.

"An act? What do you mean?"

"You're always pretending to be someone you aren't."

"I don't know where you got that idea. As Popeye said, 'I yam what I yam.'"

"Very funny, Brielle. Why won't you open up to me? You did it once."

"I did that because I'm stupid. And I won't do it again."

"Give me something more of yourself," Colt said.

"I thought I just gave you everything."

"Only in a sense. Please, give me a reason for this facade of yours."

To her amazement, she found herself speaking. Was it the way his fingers were working their magic on her back?

"I don't even know anymore, Colt. I just know that I have to protect myself." she answered.

"From who?"

"Everyone. When I get close to people, they betray me." Her eyes drifted shut as she listened to the soothing beat of his calm heart.

"It can't be everyone, Brielle. What about your family?"

She tensed, but he just kneaded her skin a little bit more, and soon her muscles were relaxing. "We used to be very close. My mother left when I was only three. I didn't know her, don't remember missing her. But I did. And when I was thirteen…"

She stopped, her heart racing as she realized what she'd almost revealed. No matter how relaxed she was, that was something she couldn't speak of — it was something she'd never told another living soul.

"Everything just changed. It didn't happen overnight. It may be something small, but I remember this well. We went from having dinner together every day to a few times a week, to a couple times a month, to never having dinner with all six of us there at the same time. Some of it was school schedules, some of it was Dad always working, and some of it was when the boys began leaving for college and the house grew more and more empty. But somewhere during that time, it just stopped mattering. It was more of an annoyance when Dad would stop us and ask what was happening in our lives. The days just kept on coming and going, and soon I turned eighteen, graduated high school and left for college. Then, there was only Dad left."

"But that wouldn't tear you apart," he said with justified confusion.

"No. That was just a piece of it. It all happened so gradually, I didn't even notice it, didn't notice the walls I'd built, didn't notice my brothers doing the same. We went from breakfast and dinner together, sharing in each other's lives, to virtual strangers."

The sadness began creeping in, and Brielle didn't want it to. This moment was good, it was pure, it was about feeling something other than pain. She didn't want to think about her family, didn't want to think about how it had all fallen apart. Brielle had to change the subject, and to do it fast. "What about you? Why did your parents only have one kid? Wait! I don't even know if that's true. That's so embarrassing. Do you have any siblings?"

She was lying naked with a man who had his hands all over her body, who'd just sated her in the best possible way, yet she knew so little about him. What did that say about her? The euphoria wore off and the defenses she was so famous for began closing in again.

As if he could sense this, he continued rubbing her back and the top of her rounded behind while he spoke. "I had a little brother."

When he stopped speaking for a little while, Brielle knew what he was about to say wouldn't be good.

"He was amazing. A miracle baby, actually. My mom had a really difficult pregnancy with me, and the doctor told her she wouldn't be able to have more children. I never felt alone, though, because, like I've said, this is a close-knit community."

He was quiet again as he gathered his thoughts and Brielle began tracing circles on his chest, offering him the only comfort she knew how to provide.

"My brother came ten years after I was born, and the doctors told my mother she couldn't carry him full term, told her that it could cost her life if she went through with the pregnancy. She told the doctors she would never sacrifice her child for her own life. So my father babied her, and both of us did all we could to make sure she was healthy and that she'd deliver another healthy child."

"She made it to seven months, and then her body just couldn't take the pregnancy anymore. She went into labor and there was nothing the doctors could do to stop it. My brother was born weighing only three pounds, but technology had already come so far by then that he had a fighting chance. His name was Blake. We practically lived at the hospital over the next two months, and I was so proud when I would get to hold him, sitting in the NICU. He was a fighter, right from the start. And it was difficult on Mom, but she was a fighter too, and it looked as if everything was going to work out with a happy ending despite everything the doctors had said."

He paused again, and Brielle's heart tightened, anticipating what was coming next. He'd said he *had* a brother, not that he still did.

"Finally, Blake got to come home. He weighed five and a half pounds and had little wisps of dark hair on his head. His eyes were blue, but mom said that could change. I didn't care. He was perfect. The first month was amazing. I had a little brother, and I adored him."

Colt collected himself to finish the story. Brielle desperately wanted to stop him, wanted this to be over with a happy ending, but hadn't she learned long ago that happy endings were made only for fairy tales?

"He was six months old, nothing wrong with him medically. His medical check-ups were great, he was healthy, and he should have had a long life ahead of him. But then one night my mother woke us up screaming. Dad made it to the room first, and I wasn't far behind. Mom held Blake in her arms while she was sobbing into the phone for an ambulance, but it was already too late..."

His scratchy voice was her undoing, and more tears fell from Brielle's eyes. She didn't want to ask, but she couldn't stop herself. "What happened?"

"Blake was already dead. He was taken in to the hospital, and tests were ran, but there never was an answer. He died in his sleep. They called it SIDS — sudden infant death syndrome. I searched and searched and searched for answers for years. Our home was safe; it was healthy. I needed an answer and I never got one. He just came and went too fast..."

"Oh, Colt. I'm...I'm so sorry." What else could she say? Nothing. There was nothing a person could say to make this better. It was never okay to lose a baby — never.

"My mom, after months of devastation, came to me one day and the two of us walked to my brother's grave — such a small grave, such a small casket they'd buried him in. But we walked there and she had a watery smile as she looked up to the heavens. I'll never forget that moment," he said, and she felt a warm teardrop fall on her forehead.

"She said, "Thank you for giving me such a gift. I know it must have been hard for you to let him leave your side, even for the six months I was blessed to have him, but thank you for those six months."

"Oh my gosh, Colt." Brielle could say nothing more than that.

"Though my brother was never forgotten, we all finally found a measure of peace."

She cried for what he had gone through. This was too much — it was all too much. Colt had found a way into her heart, and she was afraid she wouldn't be able to repair the damage to the wall she'd spent so many years building.

That was her last thought before sleep gave her some respite from the pain she knew would come her way.

CHAPTER FOURTEEN

COLT HELD BRIELLE close for much longer than he normally held a woman after sex. For some reason he couldn't seem to talk himself into letting her go. After he'd shared something with her he hadn't been planning on sharing, she had drifted off. He'd felt her body tremble with the sorrow she'd felt as he spoke of Blake, and that had torn him in half.

It was a long time ago, but not something he would ever forget, and not something he normally told anyone. It seemed he wanted to open up with Brielle, a woman he hadn't thought would ever be able to get beneath his thick skin. He knew they were all wrong for each other.

Then why did it feel so right holding her in his arms. He normally never slept with a woman after sex, but this time he'd decided to close his eyes for only a brief moment. An hour later, he woke up and she was still lying half on top of him. He felt his body stirring again just from the feel of her perfect breasts pressing against his flesh.

For a second, or maybe five, he thought about flipping her onto her back and sinking back inside her heat, finding solace in her arms. Before he could act on that, he reined himself in. This had gotten far heavier than he'd wanted it to already.

Making love to her had seemed like a foregone conclusion, nothing important, just a way to relieve one ache. But the reality was much different from the fantasy he'd created in his head. The reality was much, much better. And she'd made him want to share some of his past with her. Now he was panicking.

He couldn't want this woman for more than a single romp in the sheets. She was the enemy. She was standing between him and something he really wanted — something he deserved.

There was nowhere for their relationship to go. Nowhere good, anyway. This would only end in disaster for both of them. He knew that beyond a shadow of a doubt, so the smartest and best thing he could do for both of them was to climb out of the bed and disappear.

Wait her out.

Okay, that thought didn't particularly appeal to him. But wasn't that more than enough reason for him to get moving? Careful not to wake her, he began inching away from beneath her, untangling their limbs as he crawled from the bed.

When he stood up and looked down at her, his heart pounded at the way she grumbled in her sleep and her arm reached out. Was she seeking him out, even while unconscious? That's what it looked like. After a few seconds, she settled back into a deep sleep, and he carefully pulled the covers up over her and removed temptation from his sight.

And yet, a minute later, he found his eyes caressing her face. Yeah, he had to get away from here, because everything inside him told him not to leave and that was more than enough reason to run as fast as he could.

With fierce determination, Colt turned and began gathering his clothes. Putting on his still-damp jeans was a little more difficult than it had been to pull them off, but a few minutes later he was fully dressed.

He couldn't walk away without looking down at her peaceful face one last time. He knew that once he stepped from this room, everything would be different. All for the best, though. He quietly opened her bedroom door, slipped out, and closed it gently behind him.

When he emerged from her house, all the men were gone, thankfully. It was only about two in the afternoon and he hadn't been thinking about her reputation, or about the fact that each of the ranch hands would know exactly what he and Brielle had been up to.

He hung his head in shame at what they would now say about her. He hoped he'd be able to quash any rumors, but just as he started heading toward the barn, his cell phone rang. Looking down at the number, he sighed. This was a call he couldn't ignore.

"Hello, Tim. What can I do for you?"

He listened to his business manager for several minutes and then cursed. This was definitely not the time to be traveling. He'd walked away from her bed without a word, but he had planned to see her tomorrow. Yes, he wanted distance, but he didn't want her to feel completely used.

But wouldn't that actually help him? Wouldn't she hate him, think he was a monster? Wasn't that best for the two of them right now?

"Okay. I'll be there this evening."

He dialed another number. "Meet me at the airport," Colt said. "We're heading out."

Colt went toward his truck and made his way to the small airport in Sterling, where his collection of aircrafts was stored. He didn't get to fly nearly as much as he'd like to anymore. Sometimes because of the unpredictable weather, and sometimes because life just got in the way.

Yes, he had men who worked for him, and yes, he could do whatever he wanted to do, but Colt hadn't been raised that way. His father had worked relentlessly until the day he died, and he'd taught Colt the value of a hard day's work.

It was something so drummed into him that it would be impossible for him to do anything less than his best. Sure, he'd been spending too much time on Brielle's ranch lately, but that was work, too. He was working to obtain her land. *Hell.* Another pang hit him at the deception.

It didn't take him long to drive to the airport, and when he got to his hangar and opened the giant doors, a grin split his face as he took in his Beechcraft King Air 350i. She really was a beauty. His worries dissipated as he focused on his outside preflight checklist.

His father had flown him all around the States when Colt was just a young boy, and he'd caught the bug early on. He'd begun his first official lessons at age sixteen, and that summer he'd earned his pilot's license. It hadn't been enough for him.

As the years went by, he'd pushed himself harder and harder, and now he could fly just about anything. He had several private planes and jets, but this one was his baby, and she definitely got the most attention.

"Wow, you got here fast, Colt."

Colt turned to find Bradley, his co-pilot. He could fly this turbojet on his own, but it was always good to have a second pilot onboard, especially for some of his bigger planes.

"Yeah, Tim called. I need to get there fast."

"All right, let's do this." That was the reason Colt loved Bradley as a co-pilot. Not only was the man good company, but he also knew his stuff.

Running his hands along the surface of the plane, Colt made sure everything was in place and in working order.

"It looks good on my end," Bradley said before going around to the passenger side and climbing onboard. Colt joined him, and they read off the inside checklist together.

"Brakes set," Colt said.

"Throttle…idle," Bradley checked off.

"Weather…check; instruments set."

Opening the window — though no one was around, it still had to be done — Bradley yelled out, "Clear prop!"

Then Colt did what he loved best. With the throttle in his hand, he cranked over the engines, first the left, and then the right. No matter how many times he started the plane, it was still a thrill to hear the purr of her engines running.

"Props adjusted for high RPM."

"Strobes, lights, and radio on."

"Oil pressure is good."

Colt lifted the receiver and called for taxi clearance, and they made their way out to the runway. Once they got takeoff clearance, Colt gave her hell with a smile on his face, and just held on as she rushed forward and climbed into the sky.

Colt hoped he'd never lose the feeling of joy during takeoff, never forget how freeing it was to fly. His worries evaporated, and they rarely returned before he landed on solid ground again.

Though he knew better, Colt circled around the Ponderosa Pines Ranch and looked out the windows in hopes of catching just one far-off glimpse of Brielle. Thankfully, his co-pilot didn't say a word, though the curiosity in his eyes was practically burning a hole in Colt's skull.

Of course Colt didn't see her, but as he looked down at her roof, he knew she was there, maybe still sleeping in the bed he'd been in with her less than an hour earlier. No, probably not. The preflight check had taken him half an hour.

"All right, let's get on our way," he muttered, and Bradley just nodded, though he looked out his windows, surely wondering what Colt had been searching for.

That was something he couldn't think about right now. He had to concentrate on the controls of his turboprop jet. He could usually do that with his eyes tied behind his back, so to speak, but today was different.

Hell, his mind was back in a large ranch house, and in bed with a beautiful redhead. Colt only hoped that this strange yearning he had for the girl he planned to chase away would be long gone by the time he returned home to Sterling.

CHAPTER FIFTEEN

"THIS IS RIDICULOUS, Tony! No one will listen to me, and I'm tired of it. I'm about to fire every single person on this ranch."

Tony looked at Brielle with a raised eyebrow, but it was obvious the man wasn't concerned. What would she actually do if she did fire everyone? It wasn't as if she had the slightest clue on how to hire a new set of employees. And the wheat would have to be harvested in about a month, so without a crew she'd be up a creek without a paddle.

But for all Brielle cared right now, it could all rot into the ground. She was in a hellacious mood, one that had been building up steadily over the last two weeks.

For one single day it had seemed that she'd had the men willing to listen to her, but the next day — the day after Colt walked out of her room while she was sleeping off what she'd thought was an afternoon in heaven — she'd tried to talk to the guys and they were back to looking at her like the city girl she was.

Okay, she could admit that her sexy little temptation hadn't been the best idea ever. She was trying to earn their respect and she'd pulled a Daisy Duke move. *Freaking brilliant.* But it was all she'd been able to think of at the time.

Using her brains would have been smarter, because even if people thought she was some stupid socialite, Brielle knew she had a good mind.

So she had to prove that she was capable, that she was willing to work, that she was the owner of this place and it was time someone showed her how to do her job. If she ended up having to fire every single one of them, so be it.

It had been two weeks since she'd seen Colt, and though she was trying not to think about that, trying not to dwell on it, she was still hurt. They'd had incredible sex, followed by an intimate moment unlike anything she'd shared with any other person in the universe, and then he disappeared without a trace. No phone calls, text messages, emails — nothing. Not even a quick wave as he passed by in the yard. Of course not.

To top all of that off, she'd finally begun speaking to her father again, and he was going to show up in a couple of weeks. Great, and not so great. If she didn't appear to know what she was doing, he was going to be royally disappointed. A few months ago, that wouldn't have mattered to her. Now, it did matter, more than she cared to admit.

Feeling anything but confident in her new position as owner of this ranch, Brielle felt that she'd rather stay in a women's shelter than live one more day on this ranch with the men hating her, and with Colt who knew where.

"Please, Tony! I've been reading those books you gave me, and I've been working with Joe, the only guy here willing to work with me, but I still need to figure this all out." She hoped to high heaven that he'd cave in just a little.

And maybe it was working. Tony sighed and got ready to speak.

And was interrupted.

"What does a city girl know about working a ranch? Actually doing something around here might make you break a nail. You wouldn't want that to happen, now, would you?"

Brielle stiffened as a voice she knew all too well assailed her ears from behind.

Colt!

He was back, and not only back, but he'd dared to mock her with the first words spoken between them since he'd climbed from her bed. As she took a few deep breaths, she debated whether to use a choke hold on the rage consuming her or just to unleash it.

"What's the matter, Princess? Cat got your tongue?"

"That's it!" She whirled around and took menacing steps toward the miserable man who was so warm one minute and then cold as ice the next. Thank goodness she had her rage as protection — otherwise she'd have been completely immobilized by the way his jeans were clinging to him just right, and the way his shirt hugged his pecs and his abs.

But no. She didn't notice that this time, because everything was coming through as a bright, vivid, blistering red. How dare this man leave her bed, not speak to her for two weeks, and then come back and talk down to her?

"Where in the hell have you been? Do you think you get to just come and go as you please? I don't think so, Colt! You are so beyond fired."

She'd had it with this place and she'd had it with him and all the crazy feelings he inspired in her. Yes, she'd been through with Montana before she'd ever arrived, but right now, she wanted to do nothing more than take a match and burn the entire place down. If she didn't get some help real soon on making this freaking ranch work, she refused to be held responsible for the outcome.

"I don't think I'll let you fire me," he said with a cocky smile. "Nah. It's not a good day to do your bidding."

"You pompous, self-serving, worthless son of a bitch!" While speaking, she jammed her finger into his chest hard enough to make him flinch, though she didn't notice that. "If you even think you get to come around here after being gone for two weeks and then speak to me that way, you are sadly mistaken. I swear by all that's holy and unholy that I will take one of these pitchforks and drive it straight through that smile on your face."

When the stupid, *stupid* man had the nerve to laugh, she turned and made her way to the damned pitchfork. Before she was able to get her fingers around it, she felt steel arms wrap around her from behind.

"I missed you, too" was all the warning she got before he turned her around and pushed her against the wall, then lowered his head and kissed her. Her shock allowed him to keep their lips connected for a few seconds. Then her body stiffened with horror.

"How dare you?" She didn't even recognize her own voice, because it was on such a new register. "Do you honestly think you get to manhandle me? Do you think I won't rip you apart?"

Some of her anger drained as she looked at him. Yes, he turned her on — not at this moment, but obviously he'd gotten to her a couple weeks ago. But that didn't matter. He had no right to grab her that way, not after the way he'd treated her.

"Sorry I haven't called, sweetheart. I was stuck in Seattle for the past couple of weeks. It's too boring to even talk about." He threw her a sheepish grin as he drew back only far enough to look into her eyes, his body still pressed against hers.

Taking a moment to get herself under control, Brielle lifted her hands and pushed hard against his chest, making him take a step back. "I don't give a damn where you've been, Colt. But if you throw yourself on me like that again, you won't like the results."

"Are you upset?" The way he asked the question stopped her in her tracks. Was the man blind or just very, very dense?

"Are you really that brain-dead? Seriously? After what we did, do you think you can just disappear without so much as a word, and then strut back in here as if nothing is wrong and pick up where we left off?"

At the look in his eyes, she had the awful feeling that that's exactly what he'd thought. Counting to ten in her head, and then to twenty-five, Brielle took a few more calming breaths. Maybe all cowboys were just that clueless. How would she know?

Maybe she too was an utter and absolute fool. Because as she stood there toe to toe with him, more of her anger began dissipating. And in its place was a deep longing in the pit of her stomach. A longing that she had no business feeling. A longing to feel more of what she'd felt while in his arms. How dare he make her want him when he was so crude, so rude?

This man was trouble with a capital *T*, and she'd do best to remember that. "We're going to forget all about what happened two weeks ago," she began, and she glared when she saw the protest forming on his lips. She waited and hoped the next words from his mouth weren't as idiotic as what he'd been spouting so far.

"I can't forget what happened. I haven't for the last two weeks."

"Nope. Not going to even talk about it, Colt. If you don't release me in the next three seconds, I will be pressing assault charges against you, though."

He looked into her eyes, most likely trying to assess whether she was serious or not. When he did let her go, she felt better. At least he wasn't all-the-way foolish.

"So, Colt, where *have* you been?"

"I don't see how that's any of your concern."

"Then get out of my barn." She was dead serious. He was a slacker and she had no room for him at her ranch. She turned to leave.

"Wait!"

She paused in her step, but didn't turn around. She also didn't speak. She was waiting for his next words.

"I had family business," he finally told her.

"Are you going to tell me about it?"

"I can't." The way he said it almost constituted regret. That she could accept.

"Well, then, I guess I'll give you a break this time, and this time only, but only if you teach me what I need to do in order not to look like a birdbrain when my father gets here in two weeks."

She turned back to him, and they stood in a face-off for several tense moments. When a smile finally appeared on his lips and he lifted a hand to tip his hat, she knew that she'd just had her first small victory where Colt was concerned.

"Yes, ma'am," he said in a tone that had her narrowing her eyes.

Had it been a victory? Was he mocking her even now?

"You'll teach me?" She wanted clarification.

"I'll teach you anything you want to be taught. But you have to go along without question."

The look in his eyes told her he had a few lesson plans on the agenda that she might not be able to afford.

"Let's just keep this about business, Colt. And nothing more," she said, hoping her voice came out as strong and assured as she wanted it to.

"Brielle, nothing between us is just about business." He stepped forward so they were again too close for her comfort. When his breath rushed over her lips, a shudder ripped through her, but she managed to resist him. She hadn't the least idea how she was doing it, though.

"I will *never* just follow along like some lackey, Colt. You should learn that right now. *But*," she said, "if you keep to your word and help me, I will be willing to learn anything you can teach."

They eyed each other for a little while, neither willing to back down. Neither willing to give even a single inch. This was a battle for power, and Brielle honestly didn't know which of them had more of it right then. She'd be better off without him, but then she might never be able to make this place a success.

"I'll teach you," he practically purred. "Give me time to come up with a plan." Then he edged another inch closer.

She was done with this game. She'd gotten what she wanted, and now it was time to leave. "Colt, get out of my way." Her voice was stiff. She was too afraid that if he pushed the issue, if he leaned in again and took her lips now, she would be all too willing to surrender to him.

He looked down at her as if contemplating his next move. Finally, he took a few steps back. Brielle didn't know whether she was relieved or disappointed. But as she got her legs to move and was able to walk away with minimal shaking, she decided it was relief.

Until she got into her house, that is, and flopped right down on the nearest couch. This night would most likely prove to be her loneliest one yet. Because now she knew that Colt was back. And now she knew that the feelings he'd inspired in her two weeks before weren't just a fluke.

She had no idea whether she wanted to dig herself out of the mess he brought to her life…

CHAPTER SIXTEEN

"YOU SURE YOU'RE up for this?"

"I said I wanted to learn, dammit!" She was so tired of being looked at that way. Enough was enough.

Yet two more days had passed. It was coming closer and closer to the visit her father was paying her, and Brielle was failing epically.

"All right. Just remember that you asked for it," he warned her.

"I can handle whatever you decide to throw at me, Colt." She was wearing the dang jeans, a T-shirt she wouldn't be caught out in public in, and the boots. Though she wasn't going to tell him this, they were becoming more comfortable. That was a relief.

"Here ya go, Princess."

Brielle looked at him with suspicion when he gave her a pitchfork and a wheelbarrow. "What is this for?"

"You want to work? You get to muck out the stalls. It has to be done every single day. Since you and Joe have become chummy, he's going to teach you what needs to be done."

"That's not teaching me anything," she snapped, emphasizing every word. She knew freaking well that it was a ridiculous thing for her to be doing.

"You said you'd listen to me, that you wanted to learn."

"I want to learn how to run the ranch, not do the chores."

"Chores are part of running a ranch." .

She faced him, seething. He wasn't holding his end up to the bargain, but the stubbornness in her made her decide she was going to do this. No, it didn't give her what she needed, but maybe if she did this, he would give her what she really needed.

That thought led to the wrong place in her mind, and she quickly moved on, knowing she didn't want to go there, not with Colt, never again!

When Colt walked away and Joe approached with a tentative smile on his face, Brielle sighed in resignation.

"Have you ever mucked a stall before?" Joe asked her.

At least he wasn't nearly as rude as Colt.

"No, but that doesn't mean I can't learn," she told him as he took hold of the wheelbarrow and moved through the horse barn.

"All you have to do is scoop out the messes and then we'll come in and lay fresh straw."

Brielle felt a chill go through her body. "What *kind* of messes?" When she looked down, she said with horror, "I'm scooping poop?"

Joe's cheeks turned red. She wanted to run in the opposite direction, but she knew this was some sort of test. Yes, it was a waste of time, and yes, she knew Colt was putting her in this position just because he was an ass, but she was going to do this, and do it well.

When she got a good whiff of how the horse manure smelled up close and personal, however, she started thinking this wasn't something she could do. Her stomach began heaving. Then, an hour later, her back was burning, and her eyes and nose were running. Colt had to have given her the worst possible job there was on the ranch. Joe had done three stalls to her one, and she still wasn't finished.

Every time she managed to scoop some of the disgusting poop onto her pitchfork, half would fall back off because her arms were shaking so badly. Another half hour passed before Joe declared the stall clean and pointed to the next one.

Nope. This wasn't happening, not even with her determination to prove Colt wrong about her. This crap was downright demeaning — did he really think he was being funny? She was through with Colt. It was time to hire someone who would listen to her, who wouldn't make a joke of her requests for honest help.

"I'm done," she told Joe, wiping her brow with the back of her hand as she lay the pitchfork down and moved toward the door of the barn. Guilt followed her outside, but this wasn't the life for her. She couldn't do this. Who in their right mind would choose to live like this, work so hard for so little money?

Her arms felt as if they were on fire, and her lower back ached in a way it had never ached before. She had to get away from this place. In addition to the pain radiating through her body, she was sweating buckets. Reaching up, she pushed back her hair and was disgusted when her hand came away wet.

"That's *it*."

She should go take a hot shower to ease the aches, but she was close to tears and needed to be far away from the house, from the barns, from any chance of running into anyone. That meant she was going to the lake for a swim.

Marching out to the shed, she found a quad bike that already had the key in it. Luckily, she knew how to ride one because her last boyfriend, whom she'd dated while working at the mall in D.C., had found great pleasure in the things. At first she hadn't been interested in riding, but the freedom of cruising on roads that standard vehicles couldn't handle, plus the sensation of the wind rushing through her hair, had quickly gotten her addicted to the sport.

Not even pausing to see if Colt was around, she fired up the ATV and took off through her fields. She knew the way to the lake, and she also knew that the men were occupied mending fences on the other side of the property. She knew this only because she'd overheard them talking with Tony — no, no one had actually told her. But it meant she had at least two hours before anyone would even miss her.

Upon arriving at the lake, she stripped off her clothes without hesitation, then walked out on the short dock and dove into the water, its coldness cramping her muscles for only a few seconds before a welcome sense of relief spread through her.

This was exactly what she'd needed, a day away from Tony and Colt, and from all the other little boys who were so willing to do Tony's bidding, but not hers. At some point she would learn to assert her authority, but it wasn't going to happen today.

She was just fine with that, she thought as she lay back in the water and let herself float on its surface with her eyes shut and the sun beating down on her.

She wouldn't even mind when she woke up the next day with a sunburn, because this was close to pure bliss. To hell with the wrinkles in her fair-skinned future. Before moving to Montana, she would have been terrified to swim in a real live lake, much preferring the clean but chlorinated pools owned by her family and friends. Those pools had no chance of snakes, fish, or who knew what else lurking below the surface. But, since she was in this place — did the people of Sterling have any idea what an in-ground pool was? — she had to adapt.

Her hair spread out behind her atop the water, the sweat of the day was washed away, and her limbs were already feeling better from just drifting in the pristine lake. Best of all, it was private, and she didn't have to worry about a swimsuit.

Not that she minded the tiny bikinis she owned. They were showpieces for her best assets. When she put one on, she knew she looked good, and that was a feeling any woman enjoyed having. Still, there was nothing like being in the water without even a trace of fabric blocking her from the cool goodness.

"I see you didn't really want to learn a damn thing!"

Brielle sank below the surface of the water when Colt's furious voice startled her from her "happy place."

She came back up, coughing and sputtering water. Then she turned and glared toward the dock where Colt was standing, hands on his hips and breathing fire and brimstone.

"What are you doing here, Colt? I thought you were off with the guys, that you were too busy to mess with me," she said, when she was able to speak again. Her own fury easily matched his. He had no right to be mad at her for leaving when the task he'd given her taught her nothing!

"I didn't tell you what I was doing, but when I came back to check on you, I found Joe working alone. Had I known you were going to take off at the first sign of real work, he would have had another hand to help him so he didn't have to do all those stalls by himself."

"Oh, boo-hoo. Joe is just fine! He was moving much quicker than I was. And, I didn't ask to clean up horse dung. I asked to learn how the ranch ran. We both know you gave me that task because you thought it would be funny to have the *little princess* shoveling shit. Well, you know what? I started to play your game, and then real quickly I decided you're just an arrogant ass who enjoys power trips. So I stopped." Brielle dog-paddled to stay afloat. There was no way she was swimming back toward him, not when she was naked.

"That's part of running a ranch, Brielle."

"That's crap and we both know it. Yes, it may be part of running a ranch, but I'm the owner, Colt, and there are plenty of men. That was teaching me nothing!" It was unfortunate that she couldn't face him down more effectively. Kind of hard to do when she was in the water.

"Really, Brielle? You know this because you've worked so many ranches? My dad mucked stalls his entire life, and I still muck them myself every once in a while. It's therapeutic. I figured you'd learn something and gain a deeper appreciation for how things run."

"Now who's lying, Colt? You didn't do it to teach me anything but a lesson," she contended. "And of course you muck stalls. You work for *me*. That's part of your job!"

He stopped what he was about to say, then blew out his breath in frustration before shutting his mouth. Well, too freaking bad for him. She didn't care if he didn't like her pointing out that he was a ranch hand. He could deal with it. The man acted like such a pompous jerk all the time, and someone needed to put him firmly in his place, because he was sure having fun trying to belittle her.

"You know what, Brielle? Why don't you just give this up? We both know you don't want to be here, that you wouldn't be here if it weren't for your daddy pulling your purse strings. I'm sure if you beg him hard enough, he'll let you out of this deal you're locked into with him, and then you can go back to the city…where you belong. This isn't the life for you, and we both know it, so just give up and save yourself a lot of grief."

The end of his words came out more like a sigh than as a put-down, and that hurt more than the insult. Was that what they all thought of her? That she was just a spoiled heiress with no chance of making this work? Was that why no one would talk to her, no one would teach her? They knew it was just a waste of their time.

It wasn't as if she hadn't thought about that same thing, but hearing the words from Colt, from the man she'd made love to only two weeks earlier — and knowing the other ranch hands were thinking the same thing — stung. Really stung.

Just like that, she found herself shivering in the water, her body cold and drained. This was a game she didn't want to play anymore. She was a failure, just like her father said she was, just like Tony assumed she was, and just like Colt told her she was.

Suddenly she was fighting tears. She'd held off crying for twelve years, and now she felt like doing it every freaking day. This was so not good.

"Would you please turn around? I want to get out." Her voice was weak as she struggled to keep the tears at bay.

"It's not like I haven't seen it all before, Brielle," Colt said, but this time his voice wasn't as harsh.

"Please, Colt." There was only defeat in her tone now. She hated him right now for making her face her weaknesses, for making her doubt herself. But he was right. She was failing while her brothers were thriving in their businesses. A heavy weight had descended on her chest, and if she didn't get out of this water, she never would, because her limbs were barely holding her up right now.

He was wrong in thinking that her daddy was going to save her, though. No. Her father would cast her out, and her brothers wouldn't give her a helping hand. She suddenly felt so alone, more alone than ever before. At least before this challenge her father had given her, she'd known she could come home. Now, she didn't have that same faith.

As if Colt could sense that she was at the breaking point, he turned around, and Brielle moved slowly toward the dock. He kept his back to her when she stepped out of the water, her body shaking so badly now that she could barely catch hold of her clothes.

She hadn't brought a towel, so not only did she have to put her sweaty, disgusting work clothes back on, but she'd have to put them on while she was still wet. It took her twice as long as usual, but even by the time she was finally clothed, the shivers hadn't died down. She had no idea how she'd manage to drive the quad back. She was exhausted, barely able to stand.

"Hey, are you okay?" Colt had turned back around, and as she swayed in front of him, he held out his arms and caught her. Feeling her shake must have prompted him to pull her in close against his chest.

"You're freezing," he muttered, and rubbed up and down her back.

"I'm fine," she said through chattering teeth. "Just need to get back to the house."

He pulled back and looked at her, really looked at her, and Brielle felt the unshed tears fill her eyes. She didn't want him to see her. Face it — she didn't want anyone to look at her anymore.

"Aw, hell, Brielle. I'm sorry," he whispered, and he picked her up in his arms.

She wanted to protest, wanted to tell him to stop being nice. But it was too late for that. She knew how he truly felt, and she deserved it. She needed to just leave this place, a place that made her feel so bad about herself. It had to be this place.

But instead of letting her go, he carried her over to his horse and lifted her up, barely giving her time to grip the saddle horn before he swung himself into the saddle behind her, and then wrapped an arm around her waist and held her securely against him.

"My quad..." she protested as they began moving.

"I'll send someone for it, Brielle." Then he was silent as the sun began setting in the sky and he directed his horse toward her house.

Brielle fell asleep with her head leaning against the hardness of his chest.

CHAPTER SEVENTEEN

WHEN COLT AND Brielle reached the house, the sun was setting, and, thankfully, no one was around. He didn't want anyone to witness him carrying her inside again. Not this time. It was either blind luck or fear, but no one had said a word to him about the first time he'd gone inside. Nevertheless, he knew Sterling, and word travels fast in a small town.

As he leapt down from the horse, Brielle woke up, though she was disoriented as he lifted her down effortlessly and cradled her in his arms. He didn't know how he'd gone from furious with her to worried, but there it was.

She leaned against him, still half asleep, as he walked through her front door, and he steadily made his way to the living room and sat down on the couch with her still in his arms. She appeared so vulnerable, and it was something in her he'd never seen before.

He hated that his words had done this to her, made this strong woman so weak — even if he knew it was bound to be temporary. She wasn't the spoiled little city girl he'd first thought she was. There was a lot more to Brielle than she wanted the world to see, and all of a sudden Colt found that he wanted to see beneath the layers of protection she'd built around herself and discover who she truly was.

"Why are you being so nice to me?"

Her question startled him from his thoughts, but she was asking and she deserved an honest answer. "I want to know more about you — the real you, not this spoiled little girl you try to show everyone."

"How do you know that's not me?" She couldn't hide the pain in her voice.

"I don't," he said, and he felt her recoil. "But I have a good feeling that it's an act, like I said a couple of weeks ago. I'd just really like to know why you feel the need to put on such a facade."

If he was honest with her, maybe she'd reciprocate. He practically held his breath as he waited for her to speak. He could feel her pulse increase. Had it really been so long since she'd opened up that she didn't know how to do it anymore?

"You can talk to me, Brielle. It won't leave this room," he vowed. "I know you don't know me, but once I give my word, I don't break it."

"You're right. I don't know you. I don't let myself know anyone," she said with a sigh.

"Why? You're obviously beautiful, intelligent, full of spirit, and that's just scratching the surface. Why do you feel you have to act like someone you aren't?"

Brielle sighed again. "Do you know that I have four brothers?"

"No. I knew you had siblings. I met your father. There was something he said about you all being spoiled and needing to grow up before it was too late. I wasn't in the best of moods when I spoke to him," Colt said. What he didn't say was *why* he'd been in such a bad mood. If she knew it was because he'd just learned that the land he wanted had been sold out from under him, she'd close up faster than a Venus flytrap with a fresh kill.

"Well, I do have four brothers. We used to be so close…" she began, then stopped to pull herself together. "My mother took off when I was only three. I guess she'd had enough of being with us. I never knew her. My oldest brothers have vague memories, but I have nothing, not even a memory of her smile from back then. I was so little. There are pictures, of course, but I never look at them. She betrayed me, betrayed us all. It was even worse because when I was growing up, all my friends had moms. I didn't understand why I didn't."

She choked up for a moment. Colt didn't say a word, just found himself holding her close to his chest while he ran his fingers through her hair.

"I miss them, you know."

"Miss who?"

"My brothers, even my dad. I never say that out loud, never admit to anyone that I miss them, that I need them. If I admit it, then I hurt, and I've hurt enough already to last me a lifetime. Before this last year I hadn't shed a single tear since I was thirteen years old."

"Not one tear? Not even when you got hurt?"

"Nope. Not a single tear."

"What was so significant when you were thirteen?"

She was silent for so long that Colt knew that whatever she was going to say would make a difference. He just didn't know which of them it would actually change.

"That was when I found my mom."

Colt sat there and waited. Something traumatic must have happened to make her feel the need to become so determined to hide who she really was. The air around them was so thick, it felt like an actual weight on his shoulders.

She started to squirm in his arms. "You don't really want to hear this, Colt."

He continued caressing her hair as he said, "I really do, Brielle. Open up to me. It will help."

"But I don't even know you."

"Sometimes it's easier to open up to someone you don't know, because there isn't that fear of being judged the rest of your life."

"I found out that my mother was living in South Carolina, and I had a friend who was vacationing in the same town on the coast where my mother lived. Dad didn't know, so when they asked if I could vacation with them, he let me go. It was summertime, and I stalled for almost the entire week before showing up at her door."

Again she paused as a sob stopped her. But she managed to swallow the tears. "She lived in this nice neighborhood. Nothing like where I lived with my father, but a nice two-story house with flowerpots on the front porch. It's funny the things I remember, but I clearly recall those blue ceramic pots with purple flowers in them. I gazed at them for what had to be five minutes before I worked up the courage to ring the doorbell."

"Was she home?"

"Yes. She opened the door, and I was amazed. She was so beautiful. We have the same color hair, and the same eyes. It was almost surreal looking at her in the open door. She had a friendly smile on her face as she asked how she could help me. I remember my heart thumping so hard I couldn't even breathe. I don't know what I expected, but I guess I was hoping she would recognize me immediately. I mean, I *am* her daughter, but it had been ten years since she'd seen me, and it wasn't as if she'd been home all that much those three years right after my birth. Or at least that's what my brothers said."

Brielle was rambling, but Colt didn't try to stop her. He knew this wasn't easy. He began kneading the tense muscles in her shoulders.

"I told her who I was and her smile faded — it was almost in slow motion. She looked around behind me as if worried someone was watching, and then ushered me into the house. I was so happy that she invited me in. I didn't even think about the fact that her smile had disappeared.

"We walked into the living room, and I'll never forget that moment, because there was a gas fireplace against the wall, and a few framed photos sat above it. They weren't of my brothers and me, but of her with another man and two little girls, girls with the same color hair as me…"

This time when she tried to push down the sob ripping through her, it didn't work. A deep grimace of pain contorted her beautiful face as she fought against the truth of the memory.

"You can stop, Brielle. You don't have to go down this road…"

"No. I need to finish… I asked her who they were. She told me they were her children. I'll never forget the ache in my chest at her words. I turned and asked her about me, about my brothers. She said…" She stopped again.

This time, Colt didn't interrupt.

"She said that we were strangers to her, that she had never wanted us, and had only produced us to please my father. She was so cold as she spoke to me, looking right through me. I begged her to stop, to quit saying what she was saying, but she just looked right through me, and in a cold voice she told me that I was in the real world, and I'd better grow up, that she'd married for money, but money eventually hadn't been worth the misery she'd been forced to endure, that she had never loved my father, and therefore she couldn't possibly love any children he'd helped to create. She told me never to come back or seek her out again. That her new family knew nothing about us and she wanted to keep it that way. Then she ushered me out the front door and didn't even give me a chance to turn around and look at her one last time before I heard the door shut behind me. I walked away in a fog. I didn't want my friend or her parents to see me like that, so I sat on the beach for hours. So many tears...

"When the last tear fell, I stood up, walked out to the ocean water and scrubbed my face with it, burning my eyes and nose. I didn't care. I looked out at the sunset and vowed then and there that I would never shed another tear, that no one would ever have that much control over my emotions. I changed that summer. When I went back home, I saw my dad in a different light, and my brothers. I think I blamed them all for her leaving. I didn't want to blame myself, but I did that, too. Though she said it was our father she hated, I was thirteen. At that age the world revolves around you, so I came to the conclusion that it was me who'd made her run away. I never told my brothers or my dad about the visit. It was my own private hell to deal with."

Brielle fell silent again. Just as she had that summer day, she forced the tears back and retreated inside her head.

"Don't do that, Brielle. Don't let a woman like that have so much power over you. She's the one who was wrong. She's the one who missed out on your life and the lives of your brothers. You did nothing wrong. How could a three-year-old do anything wrong? Anyway, no child could ever chase a parent away. It was her choice, so don't continue to let her shape your life." Colt turned her head so she was forced to look into his eyes.

"Why do you even care?"

"I don't know; I just do."

"Then stop. I don't want anyone to care about me!"

"Yes, you do. We all need someone to care about us. It's long past time that you realized that."

"Well, I don't need you," she said, and she began wrestling with him, trying to get away.

"I think you're lying, Brielle. I think you need me just about as much as I need you." Colt was surprised by how much he meant those words. He barely knew her, but he did need her, needed her so much, it was frightening.

There hadn't been any major trauma from his past making him afraid to love, but he knew that when he did marry, it would be for life, and he didn't want to make a bad choice. He'd seen too many people do that, and then have children, and then live in misery, or get a divorce and fight for the next twenty years.

It was why he didn't stay with women for long. When he did settle down, he wanted a marriage like his parents had shared, a marriage where he wanted to fall into his wife's arms each and every night. He hadn't found a woman yet who inspired him to drop to one knee, who he could picture lying next to for the rest of his life.

But with Brielle… It was odd, but the more he was with her, even when he was angry, even when she put on her full suit of armor, it was just…different. He wanted to know more about her, wanted to be with her. The urge to run — which he'd felt so acutely a couple of weeks before —was nowhere to be found now.

Brielle kept struggling to get free. "I'm tired. I think it's time you go," she said, pulling him from his thoughts.

He was thankful for that. "That's a good idea," Colt told her, and this time he released his hold.

She stumbled from the couch and then stood across the room with her arms over her chest as she waited for him to leave. Colt knew he should just go, but for some reason, he found himself walking toward her.

He had to have one taste, had to say goodbye with a kiss. Without saying a word, he cupped her neck in his hand and bent down, gently caressing her lips with his, holding her gaze. Her quiet sigh let him know she wanted him, but now he was the one confused. Did she want him or need him? Did it really matter?

As he turned and walked slowly away, shutting the door behind him, and almost hazily making his way toward his horse, he realized that it did matter — this city girl mattered more than he cared to admit.

As he rode home, Brielle's story played over and over again in his head. This woman had been trouble from the first day he'd found her on her backside in front of her porch. A little over a month later, she was in even more trouble.

CHAPTER EIGHTEEN

BRIELLE WOKE UP early with a headache that was throbbing so violently, it felt as if her skull would split wide open at any second. That's what crying got you.

Stumbling from bed, and proceeding by feel alone, she made her way down the stairs somehow without taking a tumble, and found the kitchen. Opening her eyes and letting in light felt excruciating, so she didn't even attempt it until she had to pour a cup of water and grab her Advil container. Then she practically crawled into the living room.

She lay on the couch and waited for the painkillers to kick in. Half an hour later, she dared to open her eyes again. There was still a minor pulsing in her temple, but she could actually move without shards of pain ripping through her.

Going back upstairs, she got ready for the day. After her meltdown yesterday, she felt vulnerable, exposed. Today she was going to take some of that back. Today she would prove that she could be a good owner of this place — that even though she didn't want to belong here, she still did.

She was going to corner Joe, and she was going to learn how to run a combine. Come hell or high water, when it came time for the harvest, she was going to help do it. She would feel useful, like a part of the team, needed.

With the wall around her heart slowly crumbling, she needed to feel this way, needed to feel something other than like a spoiled brat, or like a city girl, as Colt enjoyed saying in such a mocking tone.

With dogged determination, she showered, got dressed and made her way back downstairs to brew a fresh pot of coffee. It wasn't going to be an easy day, but she planned to learn something. And whoever refused her today was going to be fired on the spot — it was just that plain and simple.

No, she didn't want to be a tyrant, but if she was going to run this place, she had to draw a line eventually, and today was that day. And that line was only inches from every single one of her employees' toes.

Stepping outside, Brielle felt good about being up just as the sun was coming over the horizon. Though she had vowed never to let it happen, she found herself moving over to the quaint rocking loveseat on her porch and sitting down.

Sipping her coffee, she took in deep breaths of fresh mountain air, and she waited for her day to begin. When she watched a rider appear over the crest of a hill, his form perfect, his horse moving quickly, she zeroed in on the man and horse.

As the man came closer, she discovered it was Colt, and a little thrill shot through her. She hadn't wanted to see him today, had wanted to run and hide after telling him her sob story, but as he drew nearer, she couldn't feel anything other than glad.

That was something she hadn't thought would happen.

When he stopped in front of her house, their eyes connected, but she couldn't tell what he was thinking or feeling from the expression on his face. Was he happy to see her? Was this business or personal? She hated that she had to wonder, hated that she even cared.

"Good morning, Brielle," he said as he dismounted. "I hope that you had a good night's sleep."

"I did, actually," she lied. "Sorry for the breakdown yesterday." She didn't know why she was apologizing. He'd been the one to push her, but it was easier to say the words than to sit there in silence while he watched her.

After taking the steps two at a time, he joined her on the rocker, pressing his leg up against hers.

"I'm glad you opened up to me. It seems no matter how whole we are, there are things from our past that stay with us. For you, it's your mother abandoning you. For me, it's the loss of my brother and parents.

Maybe it doesn't haunt us every single day — maybe it makes us a little more approachable. I don't know. I'm not a psychologist. What I do know is that I couldn't quit thinking about you last night."

At his words, she found herself holding her breath. What did this mean? She wanted to ask, but she was still so unsure of everything, and she didn't want to seem clingy, needy, emotional.

"How about we have a truce of sorts? I'll quit throwing things at you that are ridiculous, and you…" He paused as a grin split his lips. "Well, you forgive me for being an ass?"

"Hmm. I think I can do that if…" Her own lips turned up as she felt real happiness suffused her for the first time in a long while. "If you agree to muck the stalls all day." There. That was good payback. She hadn't seen him do it once, and she'd been in the barns a lot over the last month while trying to chase down Tony.

"That's just cruel. I *was* going to show you the harvesting equipment today, but if you'd rather I muck barns…" He trailed off and the slick devil knew he had her.

"I was planning on having Joe show me," she said, but she knew Colt would be more knowledgeable. The guy seemed to know how do to everything.

"Well, in that case, you seem to be all set." He kicked out his feet and slumped down, pulling his cowboy hat over his eyes and looking as if he were going to take a nap right there on her swing.

"Okay. Fine. I do want you to show me, Colt." She'd give him his small victory.

"That's a smart woman. I know all about the equipment," he said before turning to her and winking. "And I know just how to use it."

When she blushed at his words, he laughed, slung an arm around her shoulders, and leaned back again. Brielle knew she could either pull away or angle herself just a little closer.

As the birds sang their morning melodies, she decided she'd rather snuggle. If only for this moment, the two of them had a truce, and it was a truce she didn't feel like breaking. The last month hadn't been pleasant, but it was now early July, and it looked as if things were finally turning around for her, or at least beginning to.

As she lay comfortably in Colt's arms, they watched as the sun rose over the mountains, as people began to wake and walk outside, and then it was time to move. Brielle wasn't ready, but as he stood and then turned to help her up, their fingers linked together for a few moments and she felt peace.

She could leave his arms right now because she had no doubt she'd soon be back in them again.

CHAPTER NINETEEN

RUNNING THROUGH THE high grass, Brielle couldn't keep the laughter from spilling from her lips as Colt chased after her. This was one game of cat and mouse in which the mouse desperately wanted to be captured. But she wasn't about to make it too easy on the cat.

"Give up!"

"Not a chance, Colt."

She rushed around the back of the barn, and searched for a hiding spot. She wasn't quick enough. Her breath was knocked from her lungs when Colt caught up to her and lifted her into the air.

"Gotcha!" he said triumphantly before setting her back on her feet and spinning her around. Then the teasing stopped. His head descended and his lips captured hers.

For two entire weeks, they'd spent their days with him showing her how to run the ranch, and then the two of them played games during the evening and long into the night. Sometimes it was playful, sometimes passionate, and sometimes mellow. But, for those fourteen nights, Brielle had slid easily into Colt's arms without a thought of telling him no.

"It's time for bed," he murmured after this latest cat-and-mouse game, and trailed his mouth down the side of her neck.

"I was thinking about watching a movie," she teased.

He carried her the couple of hundred yards back to the house, all without breaking a sweat. Once inside, he kissed her again, and then walked to the living room couch, and the only movie playing was the one they created… All without lights, camera, or…wait, there *was* an abundance of action.

The next morning, a rare occasion when Brielle woke before Colt, she gazed down at him while he slept. She'd never actually told Colt he could stay over, but she'd also never told him he couldn't. He somehow just ended up there in her bed every night without fail.

Yes they made love — a lot of it. But some nights they sat in the living room and played board games or, yes, actually watched a real movie, or talked for hours on end. And then it was time to sleep and he was walking her up the stairs.

Neither of them had defined their relationship. Neither spoke about a future — or even a present, when it came down to it. Brielle was terrified to open herself up to this man any more than she already had, but it seemed much too late even to think about closing herself off.

She'd never actually been in a "relationship." Yes, there was the guy from college, her first lover, but that had only been a few times, and they were never a real couple. They'd just dated, and because all of her friends had gone on and on about how great sex was, she figured she ought to experience it.

When it still wasn't spectacular after a few tries, she'd decided that pairing was over and done with. The guy hadn't been heartbroken. He'd just moved on. Later, there was the man she'd met in Paris. Now that had been better sex, but afterward she'd still felt almost hollow inside. Sure, her body had been satisfied, but nothing like this. What she shared with Colt...it was something she couldn't put into words.

And so she was in bed with a man in what most would term a relationship, but she had no idea where the two of them stood. It wasn't as if she'd change her life for him. She wouldn't stay in Montana after she'd made a success of the ranch, and he was a country boy through and through.

Just thinking about this filled her with panic. She wasn't ready to put a label on what the two of them had together, but she also wasn't willing to let him go.

As she glanced at the clock and realized it was nearing nine in the morning, her heart began racing. Her father was scheduled to arrive in less than an hour, and no way in hell did she want him to come in and find Colt.

She couldn't even explain to herself what the two of them were; how could she explain it to her dad? She'd finally been speaking to her father over the phone, was finally losing some of the resentment she'd been holding on to, and she didn't want to ruin their fragile new beginning by having him think she was shacking up with a man she'd known such a short time. But the bed was so warm, and she was having a difficult time untangling herself from her lover. Wait. Was that the right word?

"Good morning."

Startled, she looked up and found those bright hazel eyes open and looking right at her, and he had a lazy smile on his lips. His arms tightened and he pulled her closer.

"No. I haven't brushed my teeth," she said, turning away.

That didn't stop him. He chuckled, and then his hand was tangled in her mussed hair and he was pulling her on top of him and bringing her mouth to his. Within seconds, she forgot all about her morning breath, and she was lost in the intoxicating scent of his masculinity.

When he released her mouth, she felt the hard evidence of his desire pressing against her core. "Mmm," he purred as he slid his hands down her back and pressed them against her behind, letting her feel the effect she had on him — in full. But she still tried to wriggle away.

"I can't, Colt. I have to get up."

"I'm already up, darling, so let's play." He flipped the two of them over so she was lying on her back with his arousal firmly — oh, so firmly — between her legs, his hips moving against hers in the most pleasurable way. If they hadn't both been wearing pajama bottoms, he'd already be inside her, and why not? She was wet and ready.

"I really can't. My father will be here soon, and I don't want him to find me in bed and tussling with you."

"You're an adult. I'm sure he knows you have sex, Brielle." He began nibbling on her neck.

"You obviously don't have a daughter. I don't think any father wants to believe his daughter *ever* has sex," she said with a small laugh as he moved down her neck and kissed the spot right between her breasts.

He paused and she nearly groaned in frustration, but pausing was what she needed him to do. She had to climb from this bed, get him out of her house, and take a nice long hot shower. It would take her the entire hour to work up the courage to face her father.

Yes, she had learned more about the ranch, but not enough. She was so afraid he was going to deem her a complete failure. She could tell herself that it didn't matter, but she knew it did. She knew that she didn't want her dad to look at her like the spoiled brat he thought she was.

For years she'd done everything she could to make him and her brothers believe she didn't give a damn, but after only a couple of months in Montana, she was rethinking her entire life. What people thought about her mattered. What her dad thought about her mattered.

This visit had to be a good one. It just had to.

"Please, Colt. I..." She didn't want to beg him, but she was so close to caving in and that would be disastrous.

He must have read her body language, because he stopped and rolled off her, then sat up, pulled her onto his lap, and held her close. The sweet embrace was almost her undoing.

"I'm sorry, Brielle. You're right." He kissed her temple while rubbing along her spine. After a few moments, he let her go, sliding out from beneath her and standing up.

"I'll get out of here so you can have time with your dad."

Was that hurt in his voice? Did he think she was ashamed of him? She would never want him to think that. "Wait, Colt!"

He had put on his jeans and was moving toward the bedroom door, but he turned and looked at her. She couldn't read the expression in his eyes, but she needed to say something. She feared that if she didn't, he might walk from the room and then she'd never see him again.

"I..." She paused, at a loss for words. "You know that I don't care that you're a ranch hand, right?"

His eyes widened as he looked at her for a second and then took a step closer. "Are you sure about that, Brielle?" His gaze seemed to burn right through her

"Of course that doesn't matter. Your working for me has nothing to do with the fact that I don't want my dad to find you in my bed. You could be the prince of a foreign country, the president of the United States, a lawyer, doctor, anything. It wouldn't matter. All that would matter was that you were in my bed. My dad already thinks so poorly of me. I just..."

Why was it that she always revealed too much of herself to this man? He, however, was oddly quiet about himself and especially about his emotions.

Heck, she didn't even know where he slept when he wasn't in her bed. Maybe if he wanted to climb into her bed again, she should make him begin sharing more with her. Yes! He was definitely going to have to start telling her things about himself, or they weren't spending one more night together.

"I think I actually believe you," Colt said as if surprised.

"I would hope so," Brielle replied, her eyes narrowing. She was sick of people judging her and thinking she came up short.

Walking back to her, he lifted her from the bed, and pulled her into his arms. "Brielle Storm, you are not what I expected," he told her with a real smile, then leaned in and gave her one solid kiss. Then he dropped her back onto the bed.

She was speechless.

"I'll leave now before I lose my good intentions and begin ravishing you," he said. Before slipping through her door, he looked back at her one more time. "I'll be back later."

And then he was gone. Brielle didn't quite know what had just happened, but she sat there in a daze as she listened to him humming all the way down her stairs. It was several minutes after she heard the click of her front door closing before she managed to get up on her wobbly legs and drift into the bathroom.

A twenty-minute shower cleared some of the cobwebs from her brain, but not nearly as many as she needed for a visit with her father. Oh well, ready or not, the time had come. She was just putting the finishing touches on her makeup when her doorbell rang.

CHAPTER TWENTY

"THERE'S A GREAT diner in town where we can have lunch."

Brielle was exhausted after spending the first half of the day with her father, showing him the ranch, and all that she knew about it. She'd had a fake smile plastered on her face all morning, and it was really beginning to wear on her.

Her father hadn't been judgmental, hadn't made her feel like less of a person, but she was trying so desperately to impress him that her shoulders were tight and her body was on full alert. What if he decided right now that she just couldn't do this?

It wouldn't take much for him to pull the plug on the whole operation. Yes, the business was in her name, but he supplied the money to run it, and she'd never be able to get that kind of capital on her own.

Before she'd arrived and even into her first couple of weeks here, she'd have been pleased if he decided to take her away from this place. But that wasn't the way she felt now. She needed to finish this, needed to see it through. She was actually learning about the ranch now, and she desperately wanted him to notice that. And it was making her a nervous wreck.

"I'd love to try the local food," Richard said with what she thought was his first genuine smile since his arrival.

"Great!"

The two of them walked toward her front drive, where his fancy rental SUV was sitting. She would give just about anything to ride in the nice leather seats and with actual air conditioning blasting from the vents, but the devilish side of her wanted to give her father a taste of his own medicine.

"We'll take my truck, Father. After all, you got it for me," she said with a wide-eyed smile.

Richard looked over at the rusty orange heap, and she could see that he had serious doubts about getting in, but she had to give the man credit. He didn't argue; he just wrenched open the troublesome passenger door and climbed up onto the ripped vinyl.

"I'm sorry, Brielle. I didn't realize this truck was in such poor condition," he muttered when she finally managed to get the engine started.

"Don't worry about it, Dad. She runs fine," Brielle said. No. She hadn't had a change of heart where the truck was concerned. She hated the temperamental thing, but if she had to endure riding around in it, she was going to make sure her father got the same privilege.

He said something under his breath that she didn't quite catch, but she just smiled as she threw the truck into drive and went down the bumpy road just a little too fast. The ride into town was a teeth-jarring one, and Brielle couldn't be sure, but she could almost swear she saw her father send up a little prayer of thanks when they parked in front of the diner.

"I hope we get a table. It seems everyone comes to town for lunch on really hot days," Brielle said, more cheery than she'd been all day. Though the only air conditioning in her old Ford was the 2-60 kind, where the wind ripped through the cab with the two windows down while the truck was traveling at sixty miles per hour, she still felt refreshed. She'd bet her trust fund that he'd never had such an uncomfortable ride in his whole life. Payback was swell.

"Business is clearly hopping," Richard said as they stepped through the doors and she took in the crowd of chattering people.

Sure enough, there wasn't a single table left. Damn. There was no other restaurant in town, so they'd have to go to the market and pick up sandwich stuff, maybe have a picnic at the town park. But it could be worse. The park was actually quite simple and beautiful, with a pretty water fountain, a jungle gym for kids, and a few picnic tables. It was always peaceful, and the breeze wouldn't make it so bad to eat outside if they found a little shade.

As they started to leave, a voice stopped them. "Brielle, come join us."

Turning back around, Brielle saw the three women she'd met in the clothing store not long after she'd arrived in town. They were sitting at an oversized booth and all gesturing for her to come over.

Oh no. What if they brought up that embarrassing incident with Colt in the store dressing room, and her father caught on? That was all she needed. But it would be more than rude if she didn't at least go over and say hello.

Taking her dad's arm, she led him to the table where three sets of clear eyes looked them both over. She prayed she'd get their names right. "Dad, I met these nice women when I was still pretty new in town. I'd like to introduce Bethel, Eileen, and Maggie. Ladies, this is my father, Richard Storm."

When the women beamed in acknowledgment, Brielle let out a sigh of relief. If she'd butchered their names, they surely would have said something.

"Please join us for lunch," Bethel said, and she scooted over to make room.

"Oh, we couldn't do that," Brielle replied. "We're going to grab something from the market."

"Nonsense. You don't want to miss out on Pamela's lunch special," Eileen told them while scooting in on the opposite side of the table. There was now plenty of room for Brielle and her father to join them, and if she said no again, her manners would be considered seriously lacking.

"We'd love to join three lovely ladies," Richard said, and he took the seat next to Bethel.

Brielle was shocked when she saw the woman's cheeks turn pink. Gosh. Was flirting in the air? Brielle just plopped onto the seat next to Eileen.

"I'm so sorry we haven't gotten back out to see you sooner, Brielle," Bethel told her. "We were planning on coming out last week and bringing you pie, but one of the ladies at church got sick, and we ended up taking care of her dogs."

"You don't have to bring me anything," Brielle replied.

"Well, of course we do, darling," Eileen said. "You're a single lady up in that big old ranch house all alone. We have to take care of you."

And now Maggie spoke. "Yes, and I want you to come over for our midsummer celebration next week. I always plan on sending out formal invites, but no one really needs them. They already know we put on a great picnic and show by our lake."

"I wouldn't want to intrude," Brielle said, shifting in her seat and more than grateful when the waitress came up and told her and her father about the special. She ordered it without much thought since she was concentrating so hard on what the women were chatting to her father about.

"Try the sweet tea. It's fabulous," Eileen said. Brielle and her father complied, and Eileen was right. It was just about the most perfect drink possible on a hot day.

"How is Colt doing?" Bethel asked with a sly look pointed Brielle's way.

Her father stopped mid-sip and looked at her. "Who's Colt?" He looked more curious than accusing, but Brielle was sure the red suffusing her cheeks didn't help her look less guilty.

"He's one of the ranch hands," she told her father before turning to Bethel. "He's fine. All the workers are great." She *really* hoped the woman took the hint she was sending.

"From the rumors I've heard, he's more than just a ranch hand," Bethel said, and Brielle hung her head. The woman obviously didn't know how to read body language. Dammit. Brielle was practically screaming at her to quit speaking.

"Tony called this morning and said that Colt was teaching you a lot about how to run the ranch. Last night, he said the two of you were working real hard and closely examining the back wall of the barn," Bethel said with innocent eyes.

Brielle sat there mortified for a moment before speaking. "Yes. Colt has been very helpful," she said quietly.

"Yes, and it seems that Peggy really enjoyed it when the two of you went shopping in her store. Of course, he was up close and personal with helping you select the right items…in the changing room," Eileen added, making Brielle's already colorful cheeks heat to the brightest scarlet.

"I didn't know what to buy," Brielle explained, hoping her father bought it.

Were these women trying to mortify her for the rest of her life, or did they really just get off on vicarious pleasure? She didn't know, but she did know for sure that she lost her appetite and wanted nothing more than to leave the diner as quickly as possible.

"Sounds like Colt is quite…useful," her father said.

She looked over at him, but couldn't tell what he was thinking. There was no way the dressing-room comment could have gone over his head, but maybe, just maybe, he hadn't put two and two together.

That's what she would choose to believe, if only for the sake of her own sanity. But from there, the conversation only got worse. How could the three women have found out about those things? It was as if they were spies or something. Maybe they had cameras set up on her property.

By the time she and her father left the diner, she was ready to find a sinkhole and throw herself in. When they climbed back in the truck, Richard didn't say anything until about halfway home.

"I want to meet this…Colt." That was all he said, but the tone of his voice filled her with dread. Ready or not, relationship or not, Colt was about to get *the talk…*

CHAPTER TWENTY-ONE

COLT WAS SITTING on his back deck, his feet up, a nice cold bottle of beer in one hand, a rich Cuban cigar in his other hand, and what looked like a beautiful sunset on its way. Sure, he'd rather be with Brielle, but he could give her some needed space.

As he took another swallow of beer, he realized he wasn't being honest with himself. If she called him, gave him the slightest indication that she wanted him with her now, he'd be on his horse, racing across their property lines and going straight into her arms.

That was the problem.

He didn't get hooked on girls…uh…women. So why was it that he hadn't slept in his own California King-sized bed for the past two weeks? Because the thought of going up to his empty bedroom and climbing into that giant bed all by himself left him with an empty feeling in the pit of his stomach. One that he didn't want to analyze too closely.

She knew nothing about him. Nothing! He'd held it all back. She still thought he was working for her. As he looked out at his gigantic backyard, while sitting on his 2,000-square-foot deck with attached hot tub and sauna, he felt a huge weight of guilt hang over his heart.

She'd told him that she didn't care he was a ranch hand. That he honestly believed her blew his mind. Colt knew she had more money in her locked trust fund than most people could earn in numerous lifetimes, but still, most women would care if they thought he had nothing.

Granted, he had more money in the bank than any of his possible great-grandchildren would be able to spend. Good investments on his parents' part, and then on his part, had given him financial security. Yes, his ranch made a decent profit, but he kept it running because he loved the land, loved the freedom of living in such wide-open spaces.

It wasn't about the dollars he earned. He didn't need to earn another cent the rest of his life. But how could a real man live that way? He had to work, had to feel a purpose to each day.

That didn't mean he didn't often live it up. He had expensive hobbies. In fact, if he hadn't already consumed a few beers, he'd be inclined to go to the airport and take one of his planes for a spin. There was nothing he liked more than the freedom of soaring across the sky, looking down at his land, at the beautiful state of Montana. Or, when he was feeling more adventurous, looking out over all the States of the Union in their turn.

He'd seen the Rocky Mountain peaks from only a thousand feet above the tallest one of them all, and he'd soared over the Grand Canyon and the Hoover Dam. He'd flown over the Cascades and the Great Plains of the Midwest. He'd flown all over the U.S., and he'd be happy to go out again tomorrow and find new places of beauty in the country he loved so much.

Colt wasn't a fool. He knew he was blessed, and he appreciated each new day. But since meeting Brielle, he hadn't felt the smallest impulse to leave town. The two weeks he'd been stuck in Seattle, his heart had been back home. He'd rushed through the business as quickly as he could, but it still hadn't been fast enough. Though he'd tried to push her from his head, she'd been lodged inside him, even back then.

Now that he'd spent so much more time with her, there was no getting her out of his head. Or from his heart, he feared.

Tossing his empty bottle into the recycling bin on his deck, he reached into his cooler and grabbed another. His workday had been a washout. They'd been tackling the barn roof, but he'd been nearly useless because of the way he kept wandering off in his own head, and after dragging his men down for about the tenth time, he'd called it a day and headed back. He was sure he'd heard a few sighs of relief as he retreated.

So then he'd punished himself by mucking stalls for several hours. All that had led him to was a stiff back and a really guilty conscience about doing that to Brielle that day, and now here he sat, still unable to find much in the way of peace, but at least looking as if he were. That's what was important, wasn't it?

"Why in the hell do you look like you just had to shoot your best horse?"

Colt didn't even need to look up — but he got his first smile since morning when Jackson Whitman approached. His longtime friend plopped down in the chair next to him, reached into the cooler and grabbed a bottle of beer, then popped off the top and took a long swallow.

"Who invited you?" Colt asked, but without heat.

"It's an open invitation," Jackson fired back. "Now tell me what has your panties in a bunch."

If Colt were forced to choose, he'd probably name Jackson as his best friend, though he was just about as close to Jackson's three brothers, Spence, Michael, and Camden. The five of them, plus Hawk and Bryson, had been inseparable as teenagers. They still hung out every chance they all happened to be in the same place at the same time. And when their friends from college, the Anderson boys, joined them, the real party began.

The world was a huge place, but their group had remained tight. Colt knew he couldn't lie to Jackson any more than he could have lied to his own mother if she were still alive.

"Girl problems."

Jackson waited for Colt to elaborate, but Colt didn't want to say anything more.

"Hmm," Jackson said after throwing his head back and taking another long swallow of his ice-cold beer. "Can't say as I sympathize — I'm smart enough not to have any girl troubles."

"You think you're too damn smart to have them, Jackson, but so did I. Now I have a woman on my mind, and she's refusing to budge."

There weren't many people in the world a guy could open up to on that subject, and although he knew Jackson would razz him, he also knew his friend would be a friend and offer any advice he was capable of.

Silence stretched out as Jackson finished his beer. Some might have taken his silence as rude, but Colt knew that wasn't the case. He knew that Jackson wouldn't say anything until he was sure of his words.

When the sun dipped behind the mountains and the sky filled with shades of blue and orange worthy of inspired master painters, Jackson finally spoke.

"Do you think she could be…you know…the one?"

"I don't know. That's why I'm so damn confused."

"Are you in love with her?"

Neither of them needed to say Brielle's name. Sterling was a small town, and everyone knew Colt was with her. He might as well go out and buy the freaking diamond ring right now — all the townspeople saw marriage as a foregone conclusion.

"I don't know." Colt hated that he couldn't come up with anything better than that.

Jackson chuckled. "Well, then, looks like you need another beer," he said, and he handed his best friend a new bottle.

Colt gave him a sardonic smile. "Yeah. So far the alcohol isn't giving me any more answers than you are."

"Well, at least it tastes a hell of a lot better than I do."

"I'll take your word on that," Colt retorted, and most of the tension he'd been feeling all day started leaving his muscles.

"So where are the tunes?" When Jackson stood up to flip on the radio to their favorite country station, they heard a vehicle pull up out front. "You expecting anyone?"

"Sort of," Colt replied. "I have no doubt about who it is." And his tension returned with a vengeance. "I got a call from the three meddlers after Brielle and her father had lunch with them. I've been expecting Richard to show up."

Colt didn't bother getting up when he heard his doorbell ring through the speaker on his deck. Anyone who was here could either come around his walkway or go away. He'd almost rather this man went away.

But no such luck. He and Jackson both turned as footsteps could be heard on the flagstaff walkway leading around the house.

"Hello, Colt."

Standing up, Colt looked down at Richard Storm, who was still at the foot of the stairs to his deck. He'd met Richard only twice, and both meetings hadn't gone particularly well. The first was when Colt had found out that the land he considered his had been purchased right out from under him. He'd tried like hell to get Richard to turn around and sell it, but the man hadn't budged.

The next meeting had been when Richard spoke to Tony about helping his daughter run the ranch. Colt was in the barn, and was in shock that the land was purchased for some spoiled city girl. By the end of that visit, he'd actually enjoyed Richard's company, but had serious doubts about the man's daughter.

"Richard."

They faced each other, but Colt couldn't read the other man, at least from his vantage point. Richard clearly knew that Colt had been seeing his daughter. Colt knew the meddlers had given Brielle's dad an earful.

After several tense moments, Richard made his way up onto the deck, and Colt had never wanted so badly to hang his head.

"So, my daughter thinks you're a ranch hand who works for her?"

Colt cringed as Richard looked him square in the eyes. What could he say? That was the long and short of the matter.

"Yes, sir." He knew he deserved to be taken behind the woodshed. Whatever chewing out Richard had come to give him, he deserved that and so much more. He'd lied to her. His day had gone from waking up in a great mood to quickly sinking into the gutter, and now to being in hell. Then Richard surprised the crap out of him when he spoke next.

"You will have to tell her the truth, because I think she's really fallen for you."

Colt didn't know whether he was more surprised by the small smile creeping up on Richard's face, or the words the man had just spoken. "That's impossible, Mr. Storm. There's no way. It's only been a couple of months..." He trailed off. He knew a lot more about her than she did about him. He'd shared some of his past, some of his present, and some of his dreams, but she knew nothing about the main thing.

"I don't know what you've done, Colt. I'm not going to hold that first visit we had against you, because the next one was better," Richard said with a smile. Then the smile vanished and his eyes narrowed. "At least I won't as long as you don't hurt my little girl."

"I can fix this," Colt said.

"We'll just have to see," Richard replied. Then as suddenly as the conversation had taken a serious turn, it switched again as he looked toward the cooler. "You know it's rude not to offer your guest a bottle of beer when you're clearly enjoying yours."

And that was the end of the conversation. Colt gave Richard a beer, and Jackson, who'd been standing by in case he was needed to rescue his best friend, returned and sat with them. The three of them watched the sky turn black and the glorious stars begin to dot the heavens.

Tomorrow, Colt would have to come up with a plan on how to win Brielle over so much that when he did have to tell her the truth, she'd forgive him. Easy as delivering a newborn calf, he thought.

If only that's what he really thought...

CHAPTER TWENTY-TWO

HER FATHER'S CELL phone was ringing, but the man was nowhere to be found. She would almost bet he was down in the horse arena exchanging wild tales with Tony again. Her dad had been there an entire week!

Yes, it had been good for her and her dad, and she believed they had a better understanding of each other, but it had been an entire week that she'd been all alone in her bed, the sheets unusually cold, her pillow too hard, and sleep elusive.

She'd slept alone her entire life, but after a couple of weeks with Colt next to her, she was now finding it impossible to have a decent night's rest without him. This was absurd. She didn't need Colt. *It was just sex*, she told herself. And now she knew how amazing sex could be, she missed the hell out of it.

To top it all off, her father had kept her so busy most of the time by asking questions and having her show him all the plans she'd made for the ranch, on and on, that she hadn't managed to sneak off and find Colt anywhere. She knew her favorite ranch hand was a busy man, but she was just so used to seeing him every day, and every night.

The visit had been good, but she was ready for her father to leave. It didn't help that he seemed to be bonding with her foreman. If her dad got too attached to the old fellow and decided never to leave, that would end her sex life forever.

No. She was a grown woman. If her father didn't go away soon, she was going to say to hell with it, march Colt right into the house and lead him into her bedroom, slamming the door behind them both. Yeah, somehow she knew she wasn't brave enough for that. It was so bad, though, that she'd even searched the Internet, trying to find out whether sexual frustration could cause permanent damage.

Nope. So far, she hadn't found a valid medical reason why she had to have sex. She did learn, however, that making love burned a lot of calories. If she suddenly became fat, she could so blame her father for preventing her from getting enough exercise.

When her father's cell phone rang for the third time, she couldn't stand it any longer. She picked it up, hit the button, and answered.

"Is Richard Storm available?"

"He's out of the house right now. Can I take a message?" Brielle looked around for pen and paper as she used her shoulder to hold the phone to her ear.

"Are you one of his emergency contacts?"

The woman sounded so efficient, Brielle was wondering whether she should salute. "Um…I don't know. I'm his daughter, Brielle Storm." What could this be about?

"One moment, please." The woman placed her on hold, and Brielle seriously considered hanging up. She wasn't her father's secretary.

When the woman came back on the line a few moments later, Brielle wouldn't know for quite some time whether she was happier she'd waited or if she wished she had just hung up.

"Yes, Ms. Storm, I do have you listed as a contact. Your father's newest test results have come in, and there's some conflicting information in them. Dr. Sorenson would like to have him come back in right away for a few more tests. Would this coming Friday work?"

"Wait. What test results?"

"For the prostate cancer."

The woman spoke as if Brielle knew all about it. Cancer? This had to be a mistake. Her father hadn't said anything about cancer. She wanted to shout into the phone, demand answers. But right then her father walked through the doorway, a smile on his face.

Brielle looked at him, really looked at him for the first time since she didn't know when. Yes, he seemed to have lost weight, but that was a good thing, right? There didn't seem to be any other signs of cancer.

No hair loss, no… Wait. She knew nothing of cancer, didn't know what the signs were.

The smile fell from Richard's eyes when he noticed that Brielle was holding his phone. Her eyes must have looked wild.

"Who is it, Peaches?"

Brielle couldn't speak, so she just handed her father his phone, barely managed to move over to the kitchen table, and dropped down into a chair.

She heard her father speaking into the phone, but it sounded more as if his voice were coming through a tunnel. Prostate cancer. That was bad, right? Didn't that take a lot of lives? Of course, all cancer was bad — it killed people every single day. But why hadn't he told them that he had cancer? Then the past year and several months slammed into her with the force of a sledgehammer.

He'd been so sad that day in his house when he said he needed them to make a difference in their lives. He'd spoken of changing before it was too late. When Brielle looked up, with tears filling her eyes, she found her father sitting next to her, his phone put away and a resigned look on his face.

She knew.

"You have cancer." It wasn't a question.

"Brielle—"

She cut him off before he could lie to her. "Don't!" she screamed, her voice coming back full force. "Why would you do this to us? Why would you make us care if you're planning on leaving us?"

"That's not what I've been trying to do."

Brielle wasn't listening. "You're going to leave us, aren't you?" When he was silent, she leapt to her feet. "Just like Mom. You're going to leave and never come back. You left us alone for years! For years, Dad! And then you bring us all together, and you make us care again! You did all of this just so you could rip our family apart permanently!"

It was easier to feel betrayed than to deal with the ache, the certainty that he was going to abandon her. She couldn't bear it. Last year, she might have been able to — she'd never know — but now, now she'd never get through this. Now that he'd thrown down this challenge, now that he'd began the process of removing the wall around her heart. Now she'd really suffer!

"How dare you, Father?"

Tears streamed down her face, but she swiped them away angrily. She wanted to hold on to the fury; she *needed* to hold on to it. She couldn't let the pain in.

"Brielle. I'm trying not to leave you," he said, approaching slowly, as if she were a frightened animal.

"Don't touch me! Don't you even think of touching me!" If he touched her, she'd surely break.

His own eyes filled with tears, but he kept coming closer.

"Brielle. I'm so sorry you had to find out like this. I didn't want to tell you, because it doesn't change what I want for you and your brothers."

He seemed to be pleading with her to understand, but how could she understand? She'd lost one parent, and now she was going to lose the other. It was too soon. Way too soon.

"No! You lied to me, to all of us." Wanting nothing more than to run and hide, Brielle looked wildly to her left and then right. She felt trapped.

Knowing she was about to bolt, Richard breached the gap between them and pulled her into his arms. "I'm so sorry, Brielle. I'm so sorry." He kept repeating that as he held on to her. She struggled against him for a little while, then gave up, collapsing into his arms as sobs ripped from her chest.

"Don't go, Daddy. Please don't go," she cried when she was able to speak again. She'd just gotten him back, just begun to let go of her anger. He couldn't leave now.

"I'm doing my best not to, Peaches. I really am."

She didn't know how long she clung to him, hoping that if she just held on tight, he wouldn't be able to leave, but eventually she had no more tears left.

When she was finally calm enough to listen, Richard explained about his cancer, told her that the first doctor had said there was nothing more they could do, but that he wasn't giving up, that he was still hopeful for a solution.

He'd been seeing a new doctor, one who wasn't as pessimistic as the last. That's what the call had been about, his last labs. He had to get back and get tested again. Brielle didn't want to let him go, but after spending the afternoon with her, he assured her that he would keep her updated. He promised he wouldn't ever leave her in the dark again.

The last promise he made her give before he left to catch his jet back to Seattle was to let him tell her brothers in his own time. It wasn't something easy for her to accept, but she understood.

Brielle prayed it wasn't the last time she would see her father — not now. Not when she was just beginning to feel as if she had a father again.

CHAPTER TWENTY-THREE

SHE WAS CURLED up on her sofa, clutching a cup of tea that had long since gone cold. Not that she noticed. Her father had called to tell her he'd made it home to Seattle, and to say one more time that he would keep her posted on his medical condition.

They'd spoken for an hour on the phone, and he'd even managed to make her smile a time or two, but the moment they'd hung up, the pain was back. He'd made her promise to keep working the ranch, to keep living each beautiful day. He'd assured her that he would be fine, that this was just another bump in the road, one that they'd one day laugh about.

She didn't see that ever happening, but what she couldn't change in this world, what she had no control over, was not something she should allow to have such force over her emotions.

So shouldn't she continue to do her best to succeed, to give him something to be proud of her for? Of course she should. Brielle assured herself that was exactly what she would continue doing — starting back up tomorrow. For tonight she needed to brood, to sit in the dark of her living room and drink her tea.

"Brielle?"

Her head snapped up. A shadow had appeared in the doorway to her living room, but it wasn't fear that had her heart racing; it was that

Colt was standing there. Though she couldn't see his face, she knew that silhouette, knew that voice, knew the feeling she had the moment he was in the room.

"I'm here," she said, a shiver running through her. She'd wanted to telephone him, to ask him to come to her, but suddenly everything about her life seemed so unsure. She didn't know whether she had the right to call him, because she didn't know what the two of them were to each other.

"Why are you sitting in the dark?"

"I..." She stopped as she realized how shaky her voice was.

"What's wrong, baby?" He was instantly at her side, sitting down on the couch and carefully removing the cold tea from her hand before pulling her onto his lap, just where she needed to be.

"My dad," she said with a sigh. There were no more tears left. In the last few months, Brielle had cried more than enough times to make up for the fact that she hadn't cried in twelve years.

She wouldn't cry again. "It's my dad. He has cancer." It was almost surreal to say those words out loud. She hadn't been able to tell her brothers, because of her promise to her father, but she had to speak about it, had to voice what she was feeling, and she was thankful Colt was there to listen.

"Oh, Brielle. That's terrible. May I ask what kind?"

"It's prostate cancer. He said there's a new treatment, and that's why he left today. He told me that the doctors are doing their best to fix it, but he doesn't want my brothers to know yet. He didn't want me to know. I answered his phone..."

"I'm sorry, Brielle."

She was relieved when Colt didn't try to offer her more than that, didn't try to make her unfounded promises that her father would be okay.

"I can't think about it anymore, Colt. I just can't. It's all I've been thinking about all day, and I'm so worn out. Please tell me something, anything to make me stop thinking about it."

Just sitting there in his arms took some of the burden away, just knowing he was there with her, that his hands were caressing her back, that his head was resting against hers. Just having him here with her meant she didn't have to be alone. That was so much better than sitting in the dark with a cold cup of tea.

Why was she so focused on the tea? Because it was something to think about other than cancer and death. It was something to worry about that didn't have a serious consequence.

"It's funny, really. You go through life worried about the smallest, most petty things, and then you're hit with something like this," she said, her voice almost a monotone. "I used to get so upset when I would get a fresh manicure and then chip my nail the same day. Or when I couldn't find the perfect purse to go with a brand new top. I was so shallow."

"You're anything but shallow, Brielle."

"I don't know, Colt. Can a person really change that much in only a few months?"

"If you want my honest opinion, I don't think you were ever shallow. I think you focused on those things because they were what you could control. You could look at your nails and see there was a problem that you were able to fix. You could focus on an outfit because there was a solution — or, if not, what did it really matter? Your mother left you and your family drifted apart. You were spinning and you did what you had to do in order to stay planted on the ground. That doesn't make you shallow, really — that makes you a survivor."

"I don't know how you see me the way you do, Colt, but it terrifies me."

"Why would that scare you?"

The way his hand was drifting through her hair was so soothing she almost forgot what she was saying.

"Because I feel that I'm going to fail you."

That was her second biggest fear. Her father had left from his visit saying how proud he was of her, and Colt saw an image of her that she couldn't see. What if both men were wrong?

When she tilted her head, the shadows restricted her view of his face, but she could still see the outline of his mouth, and she lifted her hand to trace his lips. How she loved the way he kissed her fingertips.

"I can see you, Brielle. I can see the beautiful woman you are, inside and out."

"I want to be beautiful for you, Colt."

"Do you really know why I love being around you?"

She wanted to know, but she almost feared what he would say. Still, she nodded her head.

"I love being around you because if I'm having a rough day, all it takes is one comment from you, one smile, one look, and my entire mood will change. What I feel when I'm with you is something most people will never in their life get to experience. I know this because I have friends who aren't afraid to speak about their feelings, and no one I know feels the way I do. I could be dragged out to every strip club in Montana and I wouldn't even see the strippers, I wouldn't even care to look, because now that I've seen you, no one compares. I can't get you from my head. I can't stop thinking about you. I can't stop wanting to be with you."

"You really feel this way?"

"I feel that and so much more, Brielle. You see, I think you were molded to fit perfectly in my arms. When I hold you, it's as if I still can't pull you close enough. I want to never let go. It's not just about sex — though that's fantastic," he said with what she knew was a grin on his face. "It's so much more than that. On paper we should be all wrong for each other, but the more I'm with you, the more I need to be with you. You have a distinct advantage over me, you know."

"What's that?" His words were doing for her what she hadn't been able to do all day. They were filling her heart with warmth, and taking away her pain. He was giving her the gift of himself, and she wanted to keep him for as long as she could — forever, if that were possible.

"What advantage?" she asked, tilting her head and brushing her lips against his.

"You own me, Brielle."

"Oh, Colt. I think you have it so backward."

CHAPTER TWENTY-FOUR

"BRIELLE, DARLING. WE'VE been waiting for you."

Brielle nearly stumbled as she came around the corner of her house to find Bethel, Eileen, Maggie, and Martin sitting on her front porch at the small table in the corner, glasses of iced tea in front of them, and pie ready to be served.

The pie made her mouth water instantly, but she was so exhausted that she didn't know if she'd be able to survive an interrogation from the terrible trio and their partner in crime, Martin Whitman.

As her stomach rumbled and her knees shook with fatigue, she decided she'd just have to do her best. She'd been up and working since dawn, and had spent the entire day with Joe as the poor kid had tried his best to teach her more about running a combine.

Colt had been teaching her, but today he'd been called away for another job, Tony said. It was a relief to have Joe help her with the huge machinery, because even after spending a couple of months with Colt, he still distracted her.

And when she was dealing with expensive machinery, she didn't need any distractions. By the end of her lessons, though, Joe wasn't looking too positive about her abilities with the combine. She would prove him wrong, though, because there was still a week until harvest time began, and she intended to spend time with the machine every single day up until then.

By the time those harvesters rolled out bright and early, she'd be a pro at cutting the beautiful wheat that filled her land.

"It's wonderful to see you ladies, and you too, Martin," she said as she dragged herself up the steps and sat at the table with the four of them. Her eyes went straight to the pie, which, if she wasn't mistaken, was still warm.

"I just feel so bad that we haven't been neighborly enough, dear, but you are a busy woman. The buzz around town is that you're doing an excellent job with this farm," Bethel said as she poured Brielle a glass of tea and passed it over.

No sweetener was needed, because it was fantastic. "I'm so happy to hear that," Brielle said, "and yes, I've been keeping pretty busy. I never would have imagined how difficult it is to run a farm of this size, but to tell you the truth, most days I'm really enjoying it." She couldn't help but stare while Eileen sliced into the pie.

When a piece appeared in front of her, she nearly forgot her manners and scooped up a bite. But somehow she stopped herself and waited for all the others to get a piece. When Eileen set down the spatula and picked up her fork, that was Brielle's green light to dive in.

"This is fantastic," she said after swallowing.

"It's my mother's secret recipe," Maggie said with pride. "Many people have tried to beg, borrow and steal it, but I keep it hidden in the best place of all," she added with a grin while pointing to her head.

"Well, since I can't cook worth a lick, you don't have to worry that I'd try to take it."

"I would be more than happy to give you some cooking lessons," Maggie said eagerly.

"I may have to take you up on that, since living on TV dinners and chicken pot pies isn't going to do anything good for my hips," Brielle said.

"Ah, darling, you could use a few extra pounds on your hips," Bethel told her.

Martin joined in with a snort, saying, "Ladies and their talk about weight..."

"Don't pretend you don't enjoy our conversations, Martin," Eileen told him.

"That I do, Eileen, that I do," he replied, sitting back after polishing off his piece of pie.

Brielle wasn't far behind him in finishing her piece, and though she knew she'd probably regret it later, she didn't turn down the second piece Eileen passed her way, knowing she wouldn't have something this good for quite some time.

"We're here to remind you about the midsummer party at my place on Saturday. You have to come," Maggie said.

Brielle squirmed. She still didn't know many of the townspeople and would feel like an intruder.

As if reading her mind, Bethel spoke up. "We won't take no for an answer. So many of our neighbors are really looking forward to getting to know you."

"It sounds like a very nice time," Brielle finally said. She was surprised when she realized that what she'd heard actually did make it sound fun.

Joe had been speaking about the party all afternoon, saying there would be tons of food, live entertainment, activities and a firework show. Plus, he'd told her, the young ladies always dressed extra nice when they went to a good country party. He'd been more excited about that part than anything else.

"I've never had any complaints," Maggie said. "My two boys and my daughter will all be home, too, which is always wonderful."

"In that case, I wouldn't dream of turning you down," Brielle said, knowing when she was beaten.

"I'm hoping our good friend Joseph Anderson makes it out this year, but he's been busy with his growing family lately," Martin said with just a hint of jealousy, which Brielle didn't understand.

"Yes, that man has hordes of grandchildren and great-nieces and -nephews now," Bethel said with the same envious look in her eyes as Martin was sporting. "My little Sage has been so busy with school that I'm beginning to think the girl will never settle down."

"Now, Bethel, you know it won't be long," Eileen said, patting Bethel's hand.

"You guys really love babies, don't you?"

The four elderly meddlers turned toward Brielle. Maggie was the one who spoke up. "When you reach a certain age, darling, babies are what you have to look forward, too. Imagine how empty life could be if you were all alone in this big old house with no one running through the halls or calling your name."

She said those words as if they were a fate too unbearable to even think about. Brielle had never really thought about it before, thought about growing old all alone. But as she did, the thought wasn't appealing, not at all.

Didn't everyone need a perfect match, and a forever family to lean on? Maybe not everyone needed that, but Brielle had grown up in a large family. Though times hadn't always been great, she had enough good memories from her childhood to know that having a family of her own to raise sounded pretty appealing. A son and daughter with beautiful hazel eyes looking back at her sounded pretty much perfect.

Her company stayed another half an hour, and despite her physical exhaustion, Brielle found herself a bit sad to see them leave. Yes, they liked to gossip, and they wanted to know every little detail of her life, but they were also warm and caring, and she was growing quite fond of the meddling trio and their partner, Martin.

As she climbed upstairs to fall into bed before the sun was even setting, she felt contentment with her life, contentment with this community, and contentment in knowing that it wouldn't be long before Colt joined her and warded of the chill of the night.

CHAPTER TWENTY-FIVE

BRIELLE HAD BEEN to a lot of parties in her day, but she could honestly say she'd never been to anything quite like this. Kids were chasing each other with bandanas on their heads and water guns in their hands, and were falling down dramatically when a stream of water hit them.

Laughter could be heard spilling from the mesh walls of several inflatable castles set up on the grounds. There was even a dunk tank proudly displayed; a line of females stretched out for what looked like a mile, all of them waiting just to see the shirtless men who were taking part. Helium balloons were flying, and a bottle of beer seemed to be in everyone's hands.

Open tents were placed strategically around the huge yard to offer shade to those who wanted to get out of the sun, and a live band was playing upbeat music. The longer Brielle was in Sterling, the more she realized that country life had its upsides. When Colt handed her a beer, she accepted it without complaint.

She usually didn't like the taste, but the day was hot and everyone else seemed to enjoy the stuff, so she took a pull from her Corona. Not half bad. As she and Colt neared the dunk tank, her eyes widened when she recognized the man who was taunting the teenager with the dunk-determining ball.

"Come on, Danny boy, you throw like my grandma!"

"She's here, ya know, Hawk. I think someone should go and get her to see how well she throws," someone hollered, and the words were met with widespread laughter.

Just then, Danny's ball hit the bull's-eye and Hawk splashed down into the water. As he climbed back up onto the bench with water dripping from his fine abs, Brielle figured out why all the girls were in line cackling.

"I owe Hawk a dunk or two," Colt said, stepping up to the front of the line and sweet-talking the girl standing there.

Men. Did they ever get past adolescence? Not that females were much better. Brielle couldn't help but smile as the teenager giggled, blushed and then let Colt cut in.

"He tends to have that effect on girls," Brielle said with a wink that made the girl grin at her.

"Yeah, I've had a crush on him since I think I was five," she replied shyly as she watched Colt draw back his arm and pitch.

The first ball missed, and Hawk wasn't going to let that one go.

"Yeah, Colt, that looks like the throw you pitched at our homecoming game senior year."

Colt gave him an evil smile before grabbing ball number two. "Just testing the wind," he said and then threw right on the mark, sending Hawk into the tank, and the cheers went up again.

As Hawk climbed back up, he returned Colt's evil smile. "Did I forget to mention that you're up next?"

Colt released the ball, but it went way off the mark. "I didn't sign up this year."

"Yeah, but Spence couldn't make it here. Called in to perform emergency surgery. So I knew you wouldn't have a problem filling in for him. The funds go to charity, you know."

Colt turned to Brielle. "Sorry. If I refuse, the guys will tie me to the seat of the dunk tank regardless."

She brightened up. "No problem, Colt." She couldn't wait to see him in that tank.

"You'd better have an extra pair of shorts here, Hawk."

"Of course we do," Hawk said right before the next person in line sank him, this time while he wasn't ready. He leapt out of the water, coughing as he tried to catch his breath.

"What color did you say your panties were?" Colt asked.

"Just wait," Hawk replied. "You're up in five minutes."

"My turn should only take half an hour," Colt told Brielle. "There's tons for you to do in the meantime." After he leaned down to give her a lingering kiss, the pink on her cheeks had nothing to do with the hot sun beating down on them.

"Awww, don't worry about it, darling. All the single ladies are wishing they were you right now."

Brielle turned to find Bethel and Martin standing beside her. "I… uh…"

"Yeah, Colt tends to make the ladies a little tongue-tied. Come with me, darlin', and I'll introduce you to a few more men who are bound to make you speechless."

And just like that, Brielle felt herself being dragged around and introduced to so many people at the party that she'd have no hope of remembering even half of their names. Heck, she'd be lucky to remember a single one.

When twenty minutes had passed, Brielle looked longingly toward the water tank, and tried to get a word in with Bethel. She was itching to go back over there and see Colt dripping wet with the sun pouring down on him. That time she'd sprayed him with the hose in her front yard, she'd been in too much shock to really appreciate the view.

She was now more than willing to stare all she wanted, because she had no doubt that he wanted her, and no doubt that he wouldn't mind if she took her fill. Sadly, all she was able to do was catch a glimpse before Bethel carted her off to another group of people.

"Have you met the new owner of the Ponderosa Pines Ranch?" Bethel asked an attractive couple.

The woman was a few months pregnant, at least to judge by the adorable bump on her otherwise slim body. Brielle wasn't going to make a comment about it, though — she'd learned the hard way that sometimes what looked like a baby bump wasn't one at all.

"You must be Brielle Storm. It's such a pleasure to meet you," the woman said before stepping forward and giving Brielle a startling hug. Yes, Brielle was used to the friendly people in this town, but she still wasn't used to getting a hug instead of a handshake.

The woman stepped back and said, "I'm Misty, and this is my husband, Bryson Winchester."

"Wait. Winchester? That name's familiar."

"Well, I'm sure you've met his brother, Hawk," Misty said with a laugh. "All the single women around here make sure to meet him."

"That's right," Brielle said. How had she not noticed the resemblance?

"It's too bad you're taken already. Hawk and Bryson's mother has been itching for Hawk to settle down, especially since Bryson and I got married last year, and now we have a baby on the way." Misty's cheeks glowed as she ran her hand over her stomach.

"How far along are you?" Now she could ask, Brielle thought with relief.

"Only five months. The baby is due in November."

"Congratulations," she told Misty with a smile. "It was so good to meet you. I hope we run into each other again."

When Bethel's attention was diverted, Brielle practically sprinted back over to the water tank. She arrived just in time to see a shirtless Colt pushing himself out of the water and up onto the bench, the sun glinting off his hard pecs and rippling down his washboard abs. Hunger sat low and heavy in her stomach — how she wanted to climb right in the tank with him and…

That was so not the appropriate place for her mind to wander while in the midst of so many people, especially with the sound of children's laughter all around her. What had Colt turned her into? When he looked up and their eyes met, his smile increased in wattage, and she felt her knees grow shaky.

"Come on, Brielle," Colt called out, "give it a shot. But I seriously doubt you could hit the target even if you were standing three feet away."

"Oh, Colt, Colt. That was the wrong thing to say." Brielle stepped to the front of the line, and the boy who was about to throw gladly handed over the ball.

"Don't throw like a girl," Colt taunted her.

She fluttered her eyelashes at him, then looked at the target, wound her arm back, and released. The ball flew fast and straight and sank him on the first throw. When he popped back up from the water, his eyes held a look of amazement.

"I'm proud I throw like a girl, Colt. I did tell you that I have four brothers, didn't I? I've been throwing since I took my first steps. I pitched on our softball team in high school, and I was beyond pissed off when they wouldn't let me play baseball. The girls won the district playoffs and went to state my senior year."

"I never would have taken you for a ball player, Princess." This time, *princess* was spoken with reverence.

"There's still a lot you don't know about me, cowboy." She threw another ball and sank him again, wearing a huge grin while she did so.

After Colt's turn in the tank was over, she gave him a longing smile when he stepped from the changing tent, his hair wet, his cheeks glow-ing, and his shirt hugging his damp body. Neither of them said a word as he rushed to her, lifted her in his arms and gave her an explosive kiss.

"We can either sneak off into the woods or go out on the dance floor," he whispered.

"The woods, please. After seeing you all slick and wet, I'm burning up."

That was all Colt needed to hear. Grabbing her hand, he led her away to a much more private place.

CHAPTER TWENTY-SIX

COLT FELT LIKE a teenage boy as he slipped off into the woods with Brielle. That's how she made him feel all the time, lightheaded and excited. He never wanted the days to end — or the nights.

She was passionate and stimulating, adventurous, and just all-around amazing. And how she made him feel about himself was the most thrilling of all. She made him feel invincible.

He would never forget the talk he'd been given when he was getting ready to head off to college and his dad had taken him fishing down by the lake. His father had told him that if he ever found a woman who made him believe in himself, he'd be a fool to let her go, because that was the type of woman a man held onto forever.

Colt had found that woman. He just had to make sure she loved him enough to get past the information he hadn't given her about himself. Sure, he hadn't actually lied, if he wanted to get technical. She'd just assumed he worked for her. But not telling her the truth was a lie — some might call it the sin of omission.

He pushed that from his consciousness, because they were now far enough away from the townspeople that he could ravish her, make her forget about anything other than how great the two of them were together.

He'd been playing in these woods since he was a young boy, running through them with his friends, playing cops and robbers, hide-and-seek, and so much more. Sure, he'd kissed his share of women while hiding behind a tree, but he hadn't made love even once on the soft moss that covered the ground.

He was practically shaking as he thought about stripping Brielle down. Just the idea of seeing her naked under the canopy of blue, with the sunlight streaming over her perfect curves, had Colt pumped up for action.

They reached a small pond that held a lot of memories of swimming, fishing, and swinging from the trees into the water on a long rope. This was the perfect place. It was quiet, well sheltered, and the epitome of the picturesque.

Colt turned to Brielle and lowered his eyelids. Her answering grin made his heart pound. Unable to keep her from his arms for even a second longer, he pulled her close, captured her beautiful pink lips, and felt her sigh vibrate in his mouth.

His hands slid hungrily beneath her blue tank top and moved up the heated skin of her back.

"You turn me on so much," he murmured when their lips broke apart.

"Oh, Colt, no one can compare to you, or how you make me feel."

He felt like Superman.

Lifting her tank top up over her head, he tossed it behind her and took in the lacy black bra she was wearing, her lush breasts filling it well and leaving ample skin sticking out for him to swirl his tongue across. He leaned down and sucked on her delicate cleavage, eager for a taste of her pink nipples, but reluctant to rush the moment, and glorying in that sexy bra.

His hands wandered down her back, slipped inside her soft cotton skirt, and easily pushed it down, so she was standing in his arms in nothing but her black bra and matching thong panties.

Taking a step back, he paused, devouring her with his eyes, loving the soft curve of her waist, how her perfect hips flared out just right, loving the indents on the sides of her stomach and the way the soft skin led so tantalizingly to the top of her panties.

He couldn't help but groan as his eyes traveled down her milky thighs and calves. Toned. Shapely. Flawless.

"I want to look at your body, too," she told him, and he looked back up, complete satisfaction filling him at the look of hunger and self-confidence in her eyes.

She knew how much he wanted her, and she was no longer embarrassed to stand there nearly naked in front of him. She trailed a long, slim finger down the center of her cleavage and over the quivering muscles of her stomach, spreading her legs open as she leaned back against a tree right behind her.

He wished he had a camera, wished he could capture this moment, but he knew the image would be burned forever in his mind, and all he'd have to do was close his eyes to see her like this again and again.

He threw off his shirt, then began unbuttoning his jeans, never once looking away from her. As much as he loved the bra, he now wanted it far, far away, wanted to see her breasts free and swaying before him. He pointed and said, "Take that thing off." His voice was gruff, demanding.

Her lips turned up and, without hesitation, she reached up and undid the clasp on the front, then peeled the scrap of lace away. Her breasts slid out, her nipples already hard and waiting for his mouth.

"Beautiful! You are so incredibly beautiful."

"I feel the same about you, Colt" she whispered, and her breathing stuttered as she shifted, opening her legs even more.

Both of them were so ready for each other, but Colt couldn't move. He loved the foreplay of nothing but words, of sight.

Every time with her was more exciting than the last, more adventurous. This definitely wouldn't ever end. He would make sure it didn't. Colt wouldn't let this woman go — no matter what it took.

"Do you trust me?" he asked as he stepped forward and his chest brushed the tips of her breasts. A soft sigh escaped her, and then she traced the perfection of her parted lips with her tongue, making his erection jump painfully against the tight confines of his unbuttoned jeans.

"More than anyone."

Her words gave him pause, but only for a moment. He would soon tell her the truth, but this wasn't the time. He would make this right.

"Good, Brielle. Now close your eyes."

"But I want to watch you take off your jeans."

"Close your eyes," he repeated, getting more and more hot as he changed the rules, as he took over and braced his hands on the tree on either side of her.

Without another protest, Brielle did as Colt had ordered and closed her eyes. He also had to close his eyes for a second because he was so near to falling over the edge. Picking up her small tank top, he lifted her arms just over her head and positioned her wrists on a tree branch. With quick movements, he secured her hands to the branch, and her eyes popped back open in surprise.

He'd never thought of doing something so erotic before, but he wanted to see her stretched out, wanted to see how her breasts lifted when her arms were raised over her head this way. Taking a step back, he now pulled down his jeans and fitted briefs to reveal what he was feeling. Then he gripped himself and squeezed, trying to relieve the pulsing, trying to make sure this lasted.

The excitement pouring from her eyes was killing him. "You are every man's fantasy come to life, Brielle," he told her. And he stepped forward again and kissed her bottom lip before capturing it with his teeth and nipping the swollen pout she wore.

"Then give me a real kiss, Colt."

"You're my captive, Brielle. I get to do whatever I want to you." He let his lips graze down her jaw, and then he sucked on the skin of her neck.

She didn't argue; she just encouraged him with her sighs of pleasure as he moved down, his hands lifting and holding the weight of her breasts. She wriggled against him, and against the tree at her back, and bit her bottom lip to keep the groans at bay when he sucked on her nipples.

He withdrew again just to look at her, loving the way the sun and shade highlighted her body, the way his saliva on her nipples gleamed just for him. He was going crazy from the little sounds emanating from her throat, the moans of pleasure she couldn't contain.

Dropping to his knees, he circled his tongue around her belly button and felt her stomach quiver beneath his touch. And he pulled the last piece of her clothing down her long, slender legs to reveal her satin-pink core to his gaze.

No hesitation. He lifted one of her legs, placed it on his shoulder and opened her wide for his view and taste. He ran his tongue along her hot folds, drinking in her scent, her heat, her beauty.

Writhing against the tree and against him, she moaned, encouraging him to go on. He was more than happy to oblige. His arousal pulsed with the need to take her, to push inside her heat and give himself release. But he wanted her shaking, he wanted her whole body pulsing when he thrust inside her. After a few expert flicks of his tongue, she cried out his name and her body convulsed with the power of her orgasm.

Colt didn't want to lose this moment. He stood, the effects of her pleasure glistening on his lips, lifted her legs around his waist, and drove deep inside her while her convulsions remained strong.

"Colt!" she cried as he sank all the way in, and he had to pause.

Oh so tight.

"Don't quit!" she gasped.

Colt grabbed her ass and pulled out, only to drive back inside in a move so deliciously hard that they both cried out. He lost control and began thrusting in and out, her little screams of pleasure firing him up even further — as if he needed more firing up.

And when his release came, they shared their groans in a desperate kiss. When the trembling finally subsided, Colt found himself gripping her behind so hard that she was sure to have bruises, but there was only a smile of satisfaction on her face.

"That was incredible, Colt."

"What you do to me..."

"Want to go for round two?"

Colt laughed and kissed her hard. "Woman! I may not survive you."

"That would be tragic."

He reached up and freed her hands, then began massaging the muscles that were surely aching by now.

"One day spent without you is tragic, Princess."

"Then we'd better not part."

Colt kissed her again, lavishing all that he was feeling into the kiss. But voices nearby made him panic. No one could find Brielle this way. Her beauty was for his eyes only.

Brielle didn't panic. She gave him a mischievous grin and slid her hand down to grasp his manhood. "I'm *still* up for round number two," she said. "And so are you."

"You are evil, pure evil," he told her. "But we'll have to be good just this once."

"Oh, you *were* good. We both were."

"Dammit, woman, get dressed." He found her skirt and thrust it into her hands.

Colt didn't feel at ease until all her beautiful assets were covered. And yet no one came around; the voices faded away. Still, he had to hope no one had heard their cries echoing through the woods.

Hell, he didn't actually care. All anyone could feel would be envy. And the two of them couldn't possibly hide their satisfied smiles when they made it back to the party.

CHAPTER TWENTY-SEVEN

"DANCE WITH ME."

Brielle floated into Colt's arms as the band played a song she didn't know. The twinkling lights surrounding the dance floor were reflected in Colt's eyes, and he began singing the words to her…

.... and though I make mistakes, I'll never break your heart...

The words made her melt. Okay, it was just a song, and yes, someone else had written the lines, but the look he gave her and his compelling voice brought her to tears.

When he deepened the emotion in his voice for the chorus of "I Swear," by the group All 4 One, she knew it was all over for her, knew she was head over heels, irrevocably in love with this man. She'd once wondered whether she was capable of falling in love.

Now she had no doubt. She wanted to say it. Hell, she wanted to shout it out, in front of all these strangers, that she never, ever wanted to let Colt go. As the song ended, as the two of them swayed together, her head fell against his chest, the power of their gaze too much for her to take anymore.

He was singing to her, was holding her tight, but he also held a lot back. So she really didn't know what she meant to him, and she was still too afraid to ask. Could she be reading everything wrong?

This was the insecurity that Brielle dealt with, the sadness of being abandoned at a young age by the one person who was supposed to always be there for a child. Her mother's betrayal would inevitably haunt her for the rest of her life.

And though Brielle had never had any inclination to have children, she could see Colt's child growing inside her. She could picture them as a family, and she vowed that if she was lucky enough to have that picture come to life, she would be a much better mother than the woman who'd given birth to her.

When the next song came on and it was a fast number, the rest of the people dancing cheered, and then Colt was dragging her to the front of the dance floor.

"What the heck are you doing?" she asked as he put his hands into his pockets and began moving his feet in sync with the crowd.

"Come on, Brielle. It's easy — just follow me."

And so she got her first lesson in line dancing.

Brielle was terrible at it, but no one seemed to mind, and her laughter was mixed with everyone else's hoots and hollers and *yee-haws*. She and Colt stayed on the dance floor for nearly an hour, until she was hot and sweaty and in desperate need of something to drink.

He led her to an area on the rolling lawn with blankets spread out, and he sat, pulled her down onto his lap and wrapped his arms around her waist. As the fireworks began, he kissed her neck and whispered sweet promises for later that had her heart pounding.

People all around them laughed, chatted excitedly, and cheered as explosion after explosion filled the night sky with color.

Maggie stood up on the stage when the celebration was concluding, and she thanked everyone for another great year, announced that they'd raised more than ever before for the fire department, and sent out a stern motherly look as she reminded them all to use their designated drivers.

Brielle stood up slowly, knowing that Colt would come home with her, but still reluctant to leave. She found herself wishing for a time loop in which she could replay this day over and over again.

Eventually, the two of them were going to need to talk about where they were headed. Brielle had fought being in Montana, had fought against living this kind of life, thinking she was much happier in a city where they didn't even know what line dancing was. But she had found something here in Big Sky Country, and she never wanted to let it go. She only hoped that Colt's feelings mirrored her own.

"I have to say, Brielle, that this has been one of the best days I've ever had."

"I was just thinking the same thing, Colt."

He drew her into his arms. "I know I'm probably going to scare you to death, but I love you, Brielle. I can't go a single minute without thinking about you. I can't imagine you moving away from here, leaving what we have together behind."

After a brief silence, she lifted her hand to cradle his face. "I won't lie and say I'm not terrified to say this, Colt...but I love you, too."

But was love enough? Sometimes it was, but unfortunately, sometimes it wasn't.

CHAPTER TWENTY-EIGHT

IT WAS THE first day of harvest, a process that would take weeks, and Brielle wasn't as confident as she should have been in her ability to help. But she was bound and determined to give it her best. Though she knew Joe was worried, Colt had told her that a combine was easy-peasy. It was just like driving a car, really — a really, *really* big car.

Hey, what could go wrong?

After her shower, Brielle dressed and came downstairs in a hopeful mood. The sun was just beginning to rise in the sky and she was ready to get started with the workday. Before her job at the mall last year she hadn't worked for a paycheck once in her life. She'd gone to school and she'd done a lot of service work with her brothers when she was younger, but she hadn't punched a time clock. It was one of the advantages of being raised in wealth.

So Brielle was completely surprised by how much she was enjoying running this ranch. Sure, there were some tasks and projects she despised, but she adored others, and all in all, she was happy with her large spread here in the middle of Montana.

Once she made it outside, she watched as her large crew gathered together. She didn't know whether she was relieved or sad when she didn't find Colt among them, but it didn't matter. She would prove to him today that he hadn't been wasting his time on her, that what he'd been teaching her over the last month was sticking.

"Hi, Brielle. What are you doing up so early?"

"I'm going to help harvest the fields, Joe," she said with a confident smile. If she appeared to know what she was doing, then surely the men would welcome her help.

"Are you sure you're ready?"

"You showed me what to do. I can handle this," she said, sending him a look that told him he would be unwise to argue with her. He looked as if he was about to object, but he finally just shrugged and muttered under his breath. "What was that, Joe?" she asked.

Quickly turning back to her, he flashed her a big grin. "Nothing, boss."

She knew he was being cheeky, but she couldn't prove it, so she decided to let it go. After all, they'd be working together all day.

"All right then. Let's get started."

When Tony stepped out and saw her standing there, he was wise enough not to say a word to her. "You all know what to do," he told everyone. "Let's have a productive day, because this will be a long three weeks."

And then Brielle followed the crew out to the harvesters. Man, were those machines intimidating.

It didn't matter. She could do this. Climbing up into one of the giant beasts, she tried desperately to remember how to get it going. When she started it on only the second try, she was feeling pretty damn accomplished. When the others pulled out and she was still sitting there, she picked up her pace, and soon, though the combine jumped a little, she had it moving and a satisfied grin split her face.

"You take the field on the right."

Looking down, Brielle found the CB that Joe's words had just come through. She'd never used one before, but picking up the handle, she pushed the button. "Roger that," she said and then a giggle burst from her mouth.

For some strange reason, she'd always wanted to say that. Oh, how her old friends would mock her if they could see her now. But as she sat there, she realized how vain an existence they had all led. Yes, she'd traveled to numerous other countries, lounged on beaches around the world, and sat in the VIP section of all the best clubs, but she had nothing to show for it.

Today, she was doing something that mattered. The wheat would be harvested and then used all around the world to fill bellies, to provide nourishment. That was something much more important than lying topless on the sands of Brazil.

She felt pretty dang cool sitting in this behemoth harvester. Taking a few minutes, she watched what the other men were doing, and soon, she was on the edge of the field and cutting away. As the blades on her combine knocked down row after row of wheat, Brielle knew there was no way the men could say she didn't know what she was doing anymore.

Sure, her rows might not be as smooth or straight as the men's, but that didn't matter. All that mattered was that she was out here working. She was being productive, and she was learning something new.

Halfway through the field, Brielle grew concerned. She couldn't quite put a name to the odor, but it was certainly a burnt smell. But it had to be that the machine was working so hard. Not that big a deal. She continued on for a few more minutes, until smoke began drifting inside her cab.

Panic filled her when the smoke became overwhelming. When she looked back and saw flames, she reached a whole new level of terror. She opened the door and looked down at the moving ground.

Not knowing what else to do, she jumped out and found herself rolling in the field as the combine continued moving forward with smoke billowing from the undercarriage and cabin.

Fear driving her on, she leapt to her feet and began running, looking back over her shoulder to see the combine light up on fire, and the wheat field go up like a torch. The flames reached out toward her like demonic fingers, moving closer and closer. What if she ended up burned to a crisp in this giant wheat field?

That would be the perfect ending to her perfect life, she thought as she tried to run as fast as she could through the field, disoriented as the smoke swirled all around her. Not taking the time to look back over her shoulder again, she ran as fast as she could, the smell of the smoke making her cough and causing her lungs to burn.

Then she tripped and went skidding face first into a cut row. It was the end. Struggling to her feet again, she glanced around — the wrong move.

The fire was right on top of her, flames only a few feet away. Screaming, she began running again. Was it too late already?

CHAPTER TWENTY-NINE

"DO YOU SMELL something?"

Colt looked over at Tony as the two men walked from the barn. He had his own fields to harvest today, but instead of hopping into a combine and blaring his favorite country tunes, he found himself once again at the Ponderosa Pines Ranch.

Colt was bowled over by the transformation he'd seen in Brielle. Sure, he knew that much of the way she'd behaved when she'd first arrived had been an act, but she still hadn't known a thing about running a ranch. This last month, though, she'd soaked up everything he was telling her, and she'd learned eagerly and efficiently. When Tony told him she'd decided to take out one of the combines and harvest a wheat field, he'd laughed. Not at her, but with delight.

She was doing an excellent job of learning how to run the ranch, and she wasn't happy just sitting idly by on the couch anymore. She was getting her hands dirty and she was earning the respect of her employees.

Wait. Yeah, Colt did smell something. "What *is* that?"

"It smells like burning rubber."

The two men picked up the pace and looked over the ranch. One of the combines seemed to be smoking.

"What the hell?" Tony exclaimed.

The two men stood in shock for a few seconds, neither of them moving as one of the wheat fields slowly began smoldering. Next, they saw flames shoot from the bottom of the combine, setting the smolder to a full-fledged blaze, and then the door to the combine opened and out rolled Brielle.

"Is she trying to get herself killed?" Tony took out his cell phone to call out an SOS to all local ranchers.

Colt watched the combine go up in a fiery ball while still moving in slow circles in the dry wheat field. It wouldn't take long for this blaze to get out of control.

It took him a moment to find his voice again. "Call the fire department," he shouted to one of the men outside the barn, and then he was sprinting toward the field as fast as he could, because even though Brielle was running away from the fire, she wasn't going fast enough. The blaze was in a hurry to catch her, and there was no way Colt was going to let that happen.

Leaping over a ditch, he made it to the field just in time to see Brielle face-plant, then get back up off the ground and scream. By now the field was ruined, and in the distance Colt could hear the sounds of the engines as several ranchers bringing their fire tenders in — huge diesel trucks with mammoth containers filled with water in the beds, basically private fire trucks.

One of the hands already had the Ponderosa Pines fire tender out on the field and was spraying away, but it wouldn't be enough to contain the blaze. He continued doing what he could as a couple of neighbors arrived and then the trucks soon surrounded the field. Men were jumping out to pull out the hoses and begin pumping thousands of gallons of water onto the blaze in hopes of keeping it to one field.

As those trucks began hosing the wheat, even more smoke appeared, and Colt lost sight of Brielle for a few seconds. Shouting her name did him no good, so he ran forward at full speed, making himself just about the only person running into the fire instead of away from it.

"Get out of there!" Martin Whitman shouted as he sprayed water at the leaping flames less than fifty yards in front of Colt.

"Can't. Brielle's out here," Colt shouted back. A huge plume of smoke covered his vision again, and Martin disappeared from view. Shouting for Brielle again, he heard another scream and he changed direction.

Someone upstairs must have had both their backs, because the smoke cleared in front of him just in time for him to see Brielle running forward, her eyes shut, water running down her soot-covered face. She tripped again, but Colt reached her just in time to catch her.

There was no time for words. The blaze was less than twenty yards away from them now, and the smoke was so thick, they'd be lucky to make it to safety. Holding his breath, Colt lifted her into his arms and rushed from the field just as the last couple of rancher fire trucks arrived and finished the circle on the field, all of their hoses pushing out water full force.

By the time Colt got Brielle back to the barn, the soot on her face had streaks in it from her eyes watering, and her coughing had died down just a little as fresh air filled her lungs. Colt could hear the town's fire engines rushing toward the field, but the ranchers already had the blaze under control. Still, it would be good if the paramedics looked at Brielle. She'd taken in a lot of smoke.

"What happened?" she asked, looking up at Colt with wide, fearful eyes.

"I don't know. Somehow your combine caught fire," he said. "The men have made sure that the fire won't leap to other fields, and soon they'll be able to go in and look at the machine to try to figure out how this began."

When Hawk Winchester arrived in an ambulance, hopped out with his bag, and came rushing forward, Colt tensed just a bit, but that was ridiculous. Hawk was his friend.

"We got the call from Andy. It looks like you guys did an excellent job containing the blaze," he said as he approached. "Are you okay, Brielle?"

Brielle nodded, but when she tried to speak, she started coughing again, so she sat silently as Hawk had her open her mouth and looked at her throat. After he put an oxygen mask on her for a few moments, Hawk removed it and asked a few more questions. This time she was able to answer.

"My lungs still feel as if they're on fire, and my throat is killing me, but I think I'm fine," she told him as he looked into her ears and eyes and took her pulse.

"I think you took in a lot of smoke, but you weren't burned. You'll have a cough for a few days, and it wouldn't hurt to go into the doc's office, but I don't see any major damage," Hawk assured her.

"I don't need to go to the doctor."

"Well, then, it's a good thing he makes house calls, 'cause I think he should do a better exam," Hawk said.

The two of them glared at each other for several moments before one of the ranch hands ran up. "Hiya, Hawk," he said with a smile before turning toward Colt just as Tony approached. "We figured out the problem."

"Well, what happened?" Tony demanded.

"Um..." He looked at Brielle with apology in his eyes before looking back at Tony, who wasn't amused at the delay. "The...um...parking brake was still set on the combine and, well, it overheated, and, well... you know the rest."

Dead silence greeted his words. Brielle's eyes widened and she sat up straight. "I caused this?" she gasped.

"It's a rookie mistake," the kid said in what he might have thought was a soothing voice.

"No! It's just another thing I've done wrong," Brielle snapped.

Colt didn't know what to say. He could see she was beating herself up. There was no need to lecture her on the importance of making sure the equipment was ready to go. It *had* been a mistake, and it was a pretty expensive one — the combine and field of wheat was unsalvageable.

"It's okay, Brielle. It happens," the kid said.

"No. I thought I could help, but obviously, you would have all been much better off without me," she said, getting up. "The ranch can't afford this kind of loss!"

"Really, it does happen." All of them turned in surprise as Tony reached out and placed a hand on Brielle's shoulder. "I did it once too when I was a new buck out there on a combine. I thought the boss was going to have my hide for sure. But he gave me a second chance."

Colt watched as Brielle fought against tears at Tony's first kind words to her. "Thank you," she said before she threw her arms around him and clung tightly.

At first, Tony seemed to be in shock from such physical contact. Then, to the shock of everyone there, Tony lifted his arms and hugged her in return, patting her back awkwardly. Colt had never seen the man show affection to any other human being.

"It's okay, Brielle. At least you were trying," Tony said, and she moved just a little closer.

When she finally let go, the tears were gone, and a watery smile was in their place. "I promise I'll do better," she told him.

And from the determined glint in her eyes Colt could see that she was serious.

She wasn't just looking at this job as a punishment anymore. She had been proving herself over and over lately. Colt looked around at the land he'd wanted for so long, and he said a silent goodbye to it, because now he didn't want to take it from her. Now, he wanted to help her succeed.

That was more important to him than adding an extra 10,000 acres to his deed.

"Equipment can be replaced; fields can be replanted. As long as no one is killed, it's not an unsalvageable day," Colt told her before pulling her close for a hug.

Hawk decided to ruin the moment. "Well, hell. We had a fire and no one even thought about bringing out the hot dogs."

"The barbecue begins after the harvest," Tony said. "We now have one less field to burn when it's all over."

"You burn the fields on purpose?" Brielle gasped.

"After the harvest, to get ready for a new planting season," Tony told her.

Joe piped up. "It's my favorite job!"

"How is that safe?" Brielle asked.

"You saw how quickly we subdued this fire. In the right conditions, field burning is the safest way to purify a field. Don't worry, Firestarter, we'll teach you," Tony said, and guffawed in his strange way before turning toward the men. "That's enough gawking, you guys. Get back to work."

The men scattered, and Colt found himself stepping back as Brielle moved away.

"I'm going to shower," she told them all before leaving.

"You going to join her?"

Colt turned to look at Hawk, who was laughing at him outright. "Maybe," he said with a wicked smile. Hell, why try to hide the fact that he wanted her? It wouldn't do him any good. It wasn't as if the entire town didn't know about the two of them now.

"Attaboy," Hawk said, clapping Colt on the back.

Colt didn't hesitate to follow Brielle back to her house. He'd had to face the reality of possibly losing her today.

Though she was his *now*, he had to tell her the truth, had to lay all his cards on the table, and that scared the hell out of him, because Colt didn't think he'd ever be the same without her. She was that woman his father had spoken about so many years earlier, the woman who made him feel like a better man, the woman he didn't want to spend another single day without.

CHAPTER THIRTY

BRIELLE STRIPPED OFF her soot-covered clothes, turned on the faucet, and waited for the water to heat. This wasn't her old condo, where she had hot water on demand. Still, she was in love with her nice big walk-in shower here, and with the huge water heater. When it finally cranked up, it allowed her to shower almost forever.

When it was warm enough, she stepped under the spray and tilted her head back, feeling better almost immediately as the black ash began washing down the drain. She let the steam fill her lungs with each deep inhalation and cleanse them from the inside out, though the heat wasn't doing wonders for her sore throat. This day had been a disaster, but a few encouraging words from Tony and she already felt better.

How sad was it that she needed his encouragement to feel better about herself? But she really was trying, and not just to beat her brothers anymore. For some reason she felt that if she didn't succeed at this, she was going to fail with the rest of her life.

Not because of the trust fund, but because she'd never tried so hard at something she didn't know how to do before. She'd been drifting through life for years, almost in a fog, counting on her family name to get her out of trouble. Those days were behind her now.

Letting the hot water cascade down her front, Brielle jumped when a pair of hands circled her from behind and climbed up her slick stomach.

"I figured you'd need help washing your back."

The words whispered in her ear sent shivers traveling down her spine, leaving glorious goose bumps on all her flesh. She should tell him to leave — should be horrified that he'd invaded her personal space. But all she could feel was pleasure as Colt pressed up against her back and cupped her wet breasts, then squeezed the nipples into aching peaks.

"I didn't give you permission to come in here," Brielle gasped, but the breathless sound of her voice wasn't doing much to chase him away and she knew it. She didn't know what she'd do if he actually did leave.

When he stepped back, she started to panic, but he just leaned against the shower wall and gave her a smile that made her legs shake. Neither of them spoke as his eyes roamed over her, so with a flirtatious smile she picked up the bottle of body wash, poured a generous amount onto a washcloth, and began rubbing it over her body, all the while looking him in the eyes.

The gasps from his mouth as she took her time sudsing her breasts, and then sliding the cloth down her stomach and over her heat made her feel like a wanton woman. The pleasure shining in his eyes told her he was turned on. Of course, what was standing up between his legs also offered welcome proof.

He didn't budge as she finished with the washcloth and ran her fingers through her hair, letting the water make it cascade out before she poured shampoo on it and lathered.

Never before had she realized that the act of bathing could be such a turn-on, but as he watched every move she made, she felt empowered, beautiful, desirable.

The feel of soapy water dripping down her body and traveling over her breasts was heightening her pleasure, making her already pulsing core almost unbearably sensitive. With her gaze locked on his, Brielle poured more body wash into her hands and ran them over her breasts, the feel of her nipples being touched sending waves of pleasure lower. Then she trailed her fingers down her stomach, and again gave attention to her swollen folds as Colt's eyes took in every...single...move.

Unable to take the heat from his eyes, she turned, placed one hand on the wall, arched her back, and ran the other hand down the curve of her hip and over her rounded behind, leaving a trail of suds. Suddenly Colt was right there, his hands coming up to cage her against the bathroom wall. "You are unbelievably sexy," he whispered, his head bent close to her ear as the water descended over them both.

He lowered one of his hands and smoothed over her stomach, seductively bending her over so that he was positioned just right for his arousal to wedge itself between her legs and rub against the outside of her core, hitting just the right place to stoke her fire even higher.

"Colt..." she cried out as he began kissing the back of her neck.

He moved his hips, letting his length rub her sensitive core, hitting her swollen pink pearl again and again while he massaged one breast, applying the perfect pressure as he pinched the nipple.

"I don't think you've gotten clean enough," he told her as he grabbed the body wash and poured some on his hands, then held her tightly below her breasts with one arm while he began moving a soapy hand across her stomach and circled her belly button before going to her core, where his hardness was still pressed.

He continued moving his hips slowly against her while his fingers moved in and began rubbing her flesh, making her cry out in pleasure as she came close to peaking. As if he could tell she was about to fall over the edge, he pulled back and shifted his fingers elsewhere on her folds, making her groan in frustration.

Between her shallow pantings, she tried to form coherent words, tried to tell him to quit torturing her. But she didn't want him to stop, because even though she wanted release, this torment he was putting her through was the sweetest of pleasure, and she never wanted it to end.

When his now suds-free fingers slipped inside her heat, with his manhood still resting along the outer edges, Brielle's knees began to buckle. Colt held her up while he stroked quickly in and out of her while sucking on her neck.

That was all it took. Release ripped through her, and he drew out the orgasm, making her body pulse against him for what seemed like hours and finally leaving her limp.

"You make me go crazy with wanting you," he groaned against her neck as his erection throbbed against her. "Feeling the force of your pleasure is beyond anything I can describe."

Brielle was shaking so much now that the weight of her five-foot-three frame was all in his arms. The sensation of his hardness still so close to her heat made her realize this wasn't over. She didn't want it to be over. Her orgasm had been more than good, but she had no doubt that with him filling her to completeness, the pleasure would be mind-boggling.

When her shaking got under control, she turned around, needing to see him, feel his lips against hers. Then she was grasping his face, pulling him to her, taking control of his mouth, with her tongue tracing his lips before slipping inside.

His involuntary groans increased her confidence, and she rubbed her breasts against his chest, pushed her stomach against the thick shaft she wanted inside her. This man was driving her to the highest reaches of heaven and she didn't want to come back down to earth ever again.

Reaching down, Brielle wrapped her slender fingers around his arousal and squeezed, making his hands grip her behind as he groaned again. She was on fire despite the water that was still raining all around them, and the slickness of their bodies together was sending her to new heights of pleasure.

She lifted one leg and wrapped it around his waist, then guided his manhood straight to her core. She was through with foreplay. She wanted him inside her, and she wanted it now. Colt's eyes widened in surprise, but he didn't hesitate as he lifted her up and braced her back against the wall.

Then, in one smooth thrust, he buried himself deep inside her heat and began pumping in and out, her folds well lubricated with her earlier release, helping him glide easily as his rhythm increased in intensity, stimulating every nerve ending from within.

Angling his head down, he buried his face between her breasts and sucked first on one side, then the other, bruising the skin slightly as he nipped it, making her cry out in passion. The sound of their wet skin slapping together only added to their delight, only added to the music of their moans echoing off the shower walls.

Brielle began panting and threw her head back against the wall while his fingers squeezed the flesh of her derrière and his erection pummeled her. "More!" she cried, urging him to go even faster. The pressure built and built until she couldn't take much more.

Suddenly, he plunged up to the hilt and then began shaking as his arousal pulsed against the walls of her core, giving her exactly what she needed for relief. As he slowed his movements and drained his hot seed into her, she attained her own release, screaming in ecstasy as she clenched against him. The orgasm went on and on.

When the last of the tremors tore through her, Brielle sagged against Colt, wondering how she would ever be able to step from this shower. Were her legs capable of moving anymore?

He swept his tongue across her breasts, just barely brushing her still-hard nipples, and a shudder rushed through her while an answering moan came from deep within his chest. There was no way either of them could come again, of course. It was impossible.

But she still clung to him, still enjoyed the feel of his hardness buried inside her while his hands held tight to her behind, and his tongue lavished attention on her breasts and neck.

"I have never felt anything like what I feel with you."

Brielle had heard these wonderful words of his before, but as he lifted his head and looked into her eyes, she had no doubt that he spoke the truth each and every time.

"I can promise you that's the same for me, Colt."

When he withdrew from her body, she whimpered, feeling bereft and empty without him. What surprised her was that he was still hard, looking more than ready to do everything all over again. Feeling a bravery she'd never known before, Brielle dropped to her knees under the shower spray, and she wrapped her lips around the thick head of his arousal before he knew what she was doing.

"Brielle!" he cried out as she took him deep into her mouth, loving the rich texture of his manhood. Though she wasn't sure whether this was doing a thing for him after the exceptional orgasm they'd just shared, she didn't care. She just wanted to feel him on her tongue, wanted to taste if there was anything left in him.

When his salty flavor hit her tongue and she felt him throb in her mouth as his pleasure built, she sighed in satisfaction. He reached down and took hold of her hair as she moved up and down his shaft. He'd given her two incredible orgasms, and she wanted to do the same for him, or die trying.

"Brielle..." he moaned as he tried to guide her head away, but she was determined to give him more. The groans erupting from his throat only encouraged her, and she moved faster and deeper along his shaft. It seemed to grow even harder; was that possible?

"I'm going to come," he warned, and she felt heat and elation rush through her body — she was able to do this for him, she was able to give him this pleasure. She sucked harder, and then she felt him begin to pulse and his fingers tighten in her hair. He cried out as he released in her mouth, a rush of warm fluid coating her tongue and sliding down her throat.

She sucked him as deep into her mouth as she could and felt a completeness she'd shared with no other man as he fell back against the wall behind him, his body spent. She finally freed him from her mouth, then sat back with a smile of supreme satisfaction. Closing her eyes and tipping her head back in the stream of water to slide her hair away from her face, she relished that she'd made this strong man weak. Talk about euphoria.

When he dropped to his knees with her, his eyes shone. "Thank you," he said before grabbing her face gently and kissing her.

That water heater couldn't quite handle this shower. The two of them didn't leave until the water was cold, and then they simply floated to her bedroom.

CHAPTER THIRTY-ONE

A WEEK LATER, COLT *still* hadn't told Brielle the truth. He knew he had to tell her. Even Tony was giving him all sorts of hell about him keeping the secret from her, because, unbelievably, Tony had grown quite fond of Brielle.

She was working hard, learning the business side of running the ranch, but also getting down in the dirt and earning sweat equity. She'd even spent a solid day mucking out stalls to make up for her first time, when she ran away, much to the delight of several of the ranch hands. Of course, she had plenty of volunteers to help her now. It helped a whole heck of a lot that she looked so damn good in her Wrangler jeans and tight cotton tank tops.

Almost since the beginning, she hadn't touched the wardrobe she'd brought with her, but Colt had seen some of it hanging in her bedroom closet, and he had plans for it. He wanted to take her somewhere she could wear diamonds dripping from her neck and ears. If he'd just get it over with and tell her who he really was, he could buy her gifts of that sort and fly her to Seattle, where they could have a romantic date, go dancing, and stay the night in a beautiful hotel.

Sleepless.

Colt had never been a man to live in fear, but the secret between them was practically eating him alive. Even Tony warned him that the longer he dragged his feet, the worse the lie became. And those feet of his were still dragging.

Every time Colt tried to say the words aloud, his throat closed. But time was definitely not on his side. He'd been amazingly lucky so far, but Brielle was becoming more comfortable with Sterling and its people, and someone was bound to say something soon. So he had to do this.

He'd planned a romantic horseback ride and picnic down at the lake that afternoon. This was the day he would spill all, he'd convinced himself. But when Brielle met him down at the barn with her jeans hugging her backside just right, and her tank top showing off her breasts to perfection, he almost forgot all about confessions — he wanted to carry her off into the hayloft and ravish her for the whole afternoon.

No. He managed somehow to rein himself in as she approached with a smile on her face — something she sported often these days.

"You take my breath away, Brielle."

"Colt, I look terrible. Don't lie to me. I was just with Joe and trying to lift hay bales. Do you know how much those miserable things weigh?"

"Yeah, darling. I've lifted a few in my day," he said with a chuckle, loving the glow in her face and that sexy-as-hell sheen of sweat.

"Well, I don't know how you guys lift them all on your own. I was determined to do anything any of the men could do, but after two hours I gave up. My arms are still shaking."

"I happen to love your arms. As a matter of fact, I wouldn't change a single thing about you."

"You might think that now, but just wait..." she said with a wink.

"There's nothing about you I don't love, Brielle."

"That's because I give you a lot of sex, Colt. You're in a sex-induced walking coma."

"Baby, if this is a coma, then never wake me up."

"Your lines have gotten much worse, Colt."

"What can I say? You inspire me."

She threw her arms around him and gave him a big kiss for his efforts. "I thought we were going for a ride."

"Not if you keep touching me like this."

"Okay, I really want to go. I think I'm getting pretty good at it now." After that mortifying fall on her first ride, she'd decided to practice in the arena. He'd watched her several times and she was picking up on it fast.

"I won't be the only one to say this, but if you put your mind to it, you can accomplish anything." He led her to Bluegrass, whom he'd already saddled.

She gave the mare a treat and petted her nose for a moment before climbing up effortlessly. "I'm getting quite fond of her," she said as she rubbed the horse's neck.

"I think she likes you, too," Colt replied as he climbed on his black stallion. Then the two of them were off, not in a hurry but enjoying the peaceful afternoon.

After about an hour of riding, sometimes spent chatting and sometimes in companionable silence, Colt said, "We'll stop here." Jumping from his horse and walking over to a favorite spot of his that boasted huge shade trees overlooking a full stream, swift and smooth, he spread out a blanket.

"I have to admit that this is almost like a postcard," Brielle said as she sat astride her horse and looked at the crystal-clear water, not quite ready to get down.

He walked back over to her. "That's one of the things I love best about Montana. There are so many areas that are unspoiled. Though the land is worked hard, it replenishes itself and stays pure."

When she climbed down from the horse, sliding against Colt, she wobbled as she hit the ground. This had been a longer ride than she was used to, and her muscles were going to be screaming at her tomorrow. Their gazes locked together and Colt forgot all about the food he'd craved just a moment earlier. Whenever he touched her, the conclusion was inevitable.

As Colt's lips moved gently across hers and his tongue played with hers, he was lost in another world, a world free of stress, a place only lovers could meet.

Several heartbeats later he pulled back, and the protest in her eyes sent a thrill through him. "I'd better feed you," Colt said with a chuckle as her stomach rumbled.

"I hope you brought something worth eating."

"Don't get me started, sweetheart. But of course I did. Every cowboy knows you don't go riding without good food in the saddlebags. You never know when you could get stuck."

"Stuck?"

"It doesn't happen very often, but when you stray too far from home base, things do occur."

He watched as she tested out her legs, made her way over to the blanket and sat down, waiting for him to unpack the goodies.

At her first bite of the juicy chicken he'd brought, she grinned. "Oh my, this is good."

"My cook is the best," he said.

His words stopped her from taking her next bite.

"Your cook? What?"

He felt his cheeks heat, and then he hated himself when Brielle looked apologetic.

"Ignore me. The cook is great," she said with a nervous laugh.

He knew she was thinking that he'd just messed up on his wording. She was assuming that the food came from the cook who prepared meals for the ranch hands. This would be the perfect opportunity for him to tell her all, but the words didn't come out, and then the moment was gone.

It was ridiculous. This was the right time. She was happy, in love, and ready to hear the truth, but no matter how he tried to talk himself into it, he couldn't say what he needed to say.

Brielle didn't notice his sudden silence — she was too busy enjoying their lunch and gazing out into the peaceful water. Maybe if she'd pushed him, he would have told her, but he didn't know. It was past time. But she wouldn't be too upset, he assured himself. Fine. Tomorrow for sure. He just didn't want to ruin their day.

That was what he told himself to make things better, at least for himself.

CHAPTER THIRTY-TWO

AFTER PARKING HER rusted pickup truck, Brielle looked back at it and tried to decide whether she had just a little fondness for it now that she'd come to terms with this country town.

Nope.

She now loved the town, but she still hated the truck. Oddly enough, it felt better that at least that much hadn't changed. Something about her hadn't made a dramatic transformation. Not that she minded what had. She felt as if she were just getting to know herself — and *like* herself.

Stepping into the salon on the small main street, she smiled broadly. It had been months since she'd had a pedicure and it was long overdue. Considering how much she'd been working, she felt not an ounce of guilt about an hour of pampering.

Brielle greeted the petite brunette in the salon with a cheerful *good morning*.

"You must be Brielle," the woman said with a sparkle in her eyes. "I'm so glad to meet you. I've only been in town a month, and the way people gossip here, I feel as if I already know you. I'm Kendra Canyon."

"It's great to meet you, too, Kendra. Yes. People do love to gossip here. At first I was a little horrified at having all my business splashed up like the front page of a newspaper or even *the National Enquirer*, but I'm getting used to it now." Brielle followed Kendra to a massaging chair that was already prepared for her pedicure.

"Take a seat, Brielle, and we'll get started. We can fill each other in on any and all gossip either one of us hasn't heard yet."

"It's been too long since I've had this done," Brielle said as she sat back and hit a button to make the chair start massaging the aching muscles in her lower back.

"That's just tragic. You have to come see me regularly. I've been so busy lately, though, that I've just put out an ad for a couple of employees. It's great, but I figured when I bought this place that it would be a little slow. I was afraid at first, thinking I wouldn't be able to make enough money to survive. I was proved wrong the first week." Kendra filled the basin with water and scented salts and then had Brielle slide her small feet in.

Another sigh escaped as the hot water soothed her feet.

"What made you move here, Kendra?" Brielle asked, although almost too relaxed to speak.

"I needed a change. I lived in Seattle and had a nasty breakup. You know, the same old song and dance we've all been through." Kendra rolled her eyes, then lifted one of Brielle's feet and began exfoliating.

"Has it been a culture shock for you coming from a large city to this place?" Brielle asked. "I thought I was going to wither up and die when I first arrived."

"It's certainly been a change, but one I wanted. I grew up in a small town in Oregon and moved to Seattle to attend college. I hated it, dropped out, and waitressed for a couple of years. Then I realized my life really sucked, so I signed up for beauty school and worked in Seattle a few years before coming here."

The two shared a few stories of their experiences in bigger cities, and an hour passed delightfully. "Please tell me you do a three-hour pedicure," Brielle said, and she was only half kidding.

"No. I think my hands would fall off," Kendra replied. "But I *am* looking for a masseuse who would be more than happy to give you a three-hour foot massage. As soon as I hire one, I'll let you know. Hold on; I'll be right back."

When Kendra returned a few minutes later with a cup of hot tea, Brielle took it happily and told her, "I can't tell you how nice this is. I love the ranch — something I never thought I'd say — but there's just something about pampering yourself that makes you feel like a woman."

"I hate to say it, but you *are* dating Colt Westbrook. You should just have him fly you to a fancy spa for the weekend."

"How would he do that?"

"Well, Brielle, the man does own like half a dozen airplanes." When Kendra turned around, Brielle's face was drained of all color.

"What?" Brielle was barely able to get that one word through her throat.

"You didn't know that?" Kendra gnawed on her lip. "I'm sorry. People just love to talk. I assumed that since you've been dating him for a while… Never mind."

"Colt works on my ranch. How could he own that many planes?" Who could afford that many? People like her father, that's who.

"I probably don't know what I'm talking about. People gossip, remember?"

"Please tell me, Kendra."

Kendra spoke reluctantly about the giant ranch Colt owned, and the huge house, planes, cars, and other toys that most people only dreamed about having. By the time the beautician was done talking, Brielle had long forgotten the sense of relaxation this visit had given her.

Brielle dug into her purse and pulled out some cash. "Thank you so much for the pedicure and the information."

Kendra refused to take the money. "Oh, this one is so on me," she told Brielle. "I'm so sorry I have such a big mouth."

"You don't — not at all. I just can't understand how I could be dating a man…hell, fall in *love* with a man who I really don't know. Why didn't he tell me? Why did he want me to think he works for me?"

Brielle's emotions were on a roller-coaster ride, going from confusion to grief, and escalating to fury in a brief amount of time.

"I'm sure he has a valid reason," Kendra said, but there was doubt in her eyes.

Was there ever an excuse for lying? Brielle wondered. Maybe at first he hadn't wanted to tell her, maybe he'd been afraid that she was a gold-digger or something like that. But they'd been making love every night and sometimes in the day, for heaven's sake. What kind of a man was he?

Brielle left the salon and walked to her truck in a daze. One thing was for sure — she wasn't waiting a single minute longer to find out who Colt Westbrook really was.

CHAPTER THIRTY-THREE

WHEN BRIELLE SAW the turnoff for the Mystic Creek Ranch, her heart lodged in her throat. His property had to border on hers. She went down the long drive, now speechless when she came up to a massive dwelling, larger than the one she'd grown up in, sitting in the center of a perfectly manicured front yard.

This wasn't the ranch of a poor man. This didn't even look like a ranch, if she were to judge by the house. Yes, the place was made of logs, but it certainly was no cabin. It was three stories high, with huge open windows. A wraparound front porch held rocking chairs, perfectly positioned flowerpots — at least they weren't blue — plus a couple of small tables, and beautiful stonework framing it all in.

This mansion cost more than any rancher should be able to afford. Colt wasn't just well-off; he was unbelievably wealthy. As she thought back to that day in her bedroom, the day she'd told him she didn't care that he was just a ranch hand, she hung her head. How he must have laughed at her as he walked away. Talk about an easy lay. A cheap date, even.

He'd been playing her this whole time, and she'd fallen in love with him. Was this something they did out here in Montana? Did they get all excited when strangers showed up so they could trot out the game *How Stupid Is the City Girl?* and guffaw?

After leaving her truck, she approached his front steps and looked cautiously at the rail. No, no spider would dare to hang out here. Why did he choose to spend every night with her when he had this home to come back to? Again, because she was easy. From the front door, she didn't hear a sound from inside the house. Then laughter drifted from somewhere out back.

Seeing a pathway, she followed it and found a gate, which opened without even a squeak. The shock of his betrayal was finally wearing off, and pure, unadulterated rage was taking hold. Why? Once she got on the other side of the gate, she saw a huge expanse of yard leading to a clear lake with a dock and a boat — and a boathouse — all waiting for the rich boy to go to and play in.

More laughter, now louder, came her way, and she followed the sound around the side of the house. Looking to her left, she found Colt on a massive deck, sitting on a chaise lounge with a cold beer in his hand, and two other men nearby.

One she recognized from the midsummer celebration — she believed his name was Jackson. The other she hadn't seen before. Oh, but the man was about to meet her, and in the mood she was in, she was sure to leave a lasting impression.

Under normal circumstances, that Colt had company might have saved him, but not this time. No. She was beyond caring what anyone thought about her. Colt had lied to her, and he was about to discover exactly why it wasn't wise to lie to the woman you claimed to love.

As if sensing her, Colt turned, and their eyes clashed. For a second or two, a smile lingered on his face, but then he sat up straighter. The look on her face had to be frightening.

"Brielle…"

Hearing her name coming from those deceiving lips drove her forward. She stomped up the stairs and didn't even bother to look at Colt's two companions. They did their best to get out of the way. Smart guys.

"Don't you dare even say my name, you lying son of a *bitch*!" She didn't even recognize her own voice.

"Brielle, I can explain."

"I'll just bet you can. Save it, Colt." She looked around the back deck of his log mansion, built-in outdoor kitchen and all. "A ranch hand? Really? You must have found immense entertainment in the fact that I thought you worked for me. Did you come home and look around and *laugh*? Was it a fun *game* for you to play?"

While he struggled to speak, she cut him off. "I lived in the world of the rich and famous for a lot of years, Colt. A *lot* of years!" she thundered. "But I will tell you this — in all that time, I never met anyone who held a candle to you. No one who came even close. With them, I knew they were lying. I knew they weren't truly my friends. That's how that world works. But bravo to you, sweetheart," she said, then raised her hands and clapped loudly. "You really *fooled* me, Colt. You got under my skin and burrowed down. You rammed right through every defense I've managed to build, and you took my heart and ran with it." On her final words, her anger drained. Despair had taken over.

Colt stood and moved toward her. "Please, Brielle. Please let me explain."

She held out her hands in horror and retreated. "Don't you dare touch me, Colt. You've lost that right!"

"I was going to tell you."

"I'm *done*, Colt. I'm *done* with you." She packed up her emotions and returned to the place she'd lived for so many years. Cold comfort.

"Don't say that, Brielle. What we have is real," he said, and took a step closer.

"No, Colt. That's where you're wrong. *We* don't have a single thing, because our relationship, or what I thought was a relationship, was built on lies. Just tell me this. Why? Was it really just a game?"

"It wasn't a game. I swear it wasn't."

She didn't know where his friends had gone, and she didn't care. The entire town knew she was a fool already.

"*Why*, Colt?"

She didn't know why it mattered, but she needed to close this chapter in her life, and the only way to do that was to have some sort of an answer.

"I didn't know you, Brielle."

"Just spit it out, Colt. I'm tired and I'm done, so just tell me."

"Your father bought the property I wanted. I didn't know you then. I wanted it, and I was willing to do whatever it took to get it," he said, and she felt like a knife was slicing into her heart. "But that changed..."

She held up her hand to keep him from saying anything more.

"It's over, Colt."

She turned and walked away. Of course, he chased after her, of course he tried to plead with her, but Brielle didn't hear a word he said through the buzzing in her ears. She didn't even see anything as she climbed into her truck and started the motor, her motions on autopilot.

"Brielle, don't leave like this," he demanded, but she was beyond listening.

Throwing the truck into gear, she drove away in a tornado of dust. She welcomed the numbness that settled over her, because she had no doubt that when the numbness vanished, the pain would be unbearable.

CHAPTER THIRTY-FOUR

A WEEK AFTER BRIELLE walked away from Colt's house, her father showed up on her doorstep, and she fell into his arms, so grateful to see him again. If she focused on her dad, she wouldn't have to focus on Colt. That's what she should be doing anyway!

There were a million questions brewing about how the cancer treatment was going. Of course they'd been in contact, and he was keeping her updated on the phone, but it would be much better to look into his eyes. That way she might know whether he was speaking the truth or trying to protect her feelings.

Anger and hurt inspired by Colt had helped to keep the tears at bay, but she simmered with frustration because the man had been showing up daily with flowers, chocolate, and jewelry, begging her to speak to him, begging her to forgive his lie. He'd offered to fly her anywhere in the world she wanted to go, offered to give up everything just for another day with her.

Of course he could give her everything money could buy. He was obscenely rich! He'd lied to her. And worse, he'd done it so that he could take her ranch from her. Colt was a user. How could she forgive that?

So it was a welcome relief to open her door and find her father standing there. She clung to him and promised herself that she was never going to let him go, that she would focus wholly on him, and not think twice about Colt Westbrook.

When Brielle looked past her father, she found two men standing beside him. At first glance, she thought nothing of it, but then her eyes snapped back first to one giant of a man, and then to the other, who wasn't far behind the first, and very close in height to her father.

The three of them looked so similar, all sporting matching white hair, identical blue eyes, and solid shoulders. Even the smiles they were each wearing looked nearly the same. What in the world was going on?

"Ha! We've been getting that reaction a lot."

One of the men spoke in such a loud voice that Brielle fell back another step.

"Honey, don't let this man intimidate you," Richard said with a reassuring hand on her shoulder. "We'll all come inside and then I can tell you everything."

Almost in a trance, Brielle nodded, and she led them to her kitchen table. She knew she should offer them something to drink, but as she looked between the three men —all so amazingly alike! — she knew her legs wouldn't work long enough to perform the whole operation. She had to sit down.

"Since we just showed up like this on your front doorstep, as we've done with three of your four brothers, I'm going to get right to it," Richard said with a gentle smile. "These are my brothers."

Brielle waited for the punch line, but when he was silent, she was forced to speak. "You don't have brothers."

"We just discovered each other after I moved to Seattle. To make a long story short, my biological mother delivered three children, triplets. Joseph and George stayed with her, and I ended up with her doctor and his wife, the nurse. We'll never know for sure if this was consensual or not, and it's better that we all not delve too deeply into it. I loved my parents very much, and that won't change. But now I have brothers, and we have much in common. Plus, you and your brothers have two uncles and a whole hell of a lot of cousins."

The joy in her father's face was contagious. Some of Brielle's recent sorrow disappeared as she watched three kindred smiles beam at her from different positions at the table.

"This is a lot to take in," she finally said.

"Well, I love that you ended up here, Brielle," Joseph told her. "There are good people in Sterling. One of my best friends, Martin Whitman, lives here, along with Bethel, Eileen, and Maggie. I'm sure you've met them all." He reached out his hand to clasp hers and added with a laugh, "I'm your Uncle Joseph, in case you got me and George confused."

"I don't think I'll mistake you with that voice," Brielle said.

"I don't understand that. Everyone says I speak so loudly. I think I'm quiet as a mouse," he replied, and she couldn't tell whether he was joking.

After the initial shock wore off, Brielle was finally able to move, so she made them a pitcher of fresh lemonade, and the four of them spoke long into the evening. Just before she went off to bed, she and her dad sat down together alone for the first time that day while Joseph and George left to visit with old friends.

"We're headed to see Crew next. He's our last stop," Richard told her. Crew and her father had probably been the ones to butt heads the most, but through this journey their father had sent them all on, the relationship of father and oldest son had improved greatly.

"I'm coming with you." Brielle didn't know the words were out until she said them.

"Well, of course I'd love to have you join us, but is it a good time for you to take off?" her dad asked.

"Yes, Tony has everything under control here, and it will only be a few days. And…" She had to fight tears. "I just need to get away for a bit."

She was more than thankful when her father didn't ask her the questions she saw forming in his eyes. "Okay, Peaches. We'll head out at first light. Don't warn your brother. We like surprising all of you. It's family drama at its best."

"I quite understand. Now enough of all of that. Tell me what your doctor has been saying."

His lips tilted up a little bit more as he looked at her. "I'm going to need to have another surgery…" he began when she stopped him by holding up her hand.

"Another surgery? When was the first one? Why would you keep this from any of us?"

She didn't want to yell at her father in the condition he was in, but at the same time, she couldn't believe that he would keep something like this from them. It was just wrong.

"I had my first surgery last year, and it didn't look good, so my previous doctor told me to get my affairs in order, which is what I set out to do with you and your brothers. Then I moved to Seattle and met my brothers. They didn't like the first prognosis and they knew another doctor, my current one. He had a different opinion. He's hopeful. I'll know more in a few months. For now, it's best for all of us to not dwell on it."

He gripped her hand as he spoke and looked at her with both hope and love in his eyes. She had a million questions, but she could see that he was tired. She'd be with him all week, and one way or another she would find better answers.

After giving her a big hug, her father went to the bedroom she kept for him, and for the first time in a week, Brielle climbed the stairs not dreading her own cold bed. She would get away, take time to think, and figure out what she was going to do next.

She didn't want to leave the Ponderosa Pines Ranch, but she didn't know how she could stay with Colt being her neighbor. Maybe she should just offer to sell it to him. That's what he really wanted, wasn't it?

She went to bed that night and finally was granted a dreamless sleep.

CHAPTER THIRTY-FIVE

COLT PACED BRIELLE'S front porch, feeling more like a fool the longer he waited. She'd been absent an entire week — she'd completely disappeared, and he had no idea where. When he first found out that she'd left, he'd thought for sure it was over, that he'd lost her for good.

Not that he would have given up so easily. Love like this didn't just disappear. No. If she moved away, he'd follow her. Even if it took months, years, decades, he would wait for her. He'd barely slept during the last two weeks, his arms empty without her in them, his heart aching without her there to fill it.

He sounded pathetic even to himself, but that was the way it was. He was desperately in love with Brielle Storm, and whatever he had to do to prove that to her he *would* do. There was no way he'd live his life without her.

He'd been greatly relieved to find out from Tony that she wasn't gone for good, but that she'd left with her father to visit one of her brothers. And Tony had let him know that she was coming home tonight.

So here he was on her front porch, where he'd been waiting for the last three hours. The ranch hands had all walked by at some point or other to snicker or just enjoy the show. Colt didn't care. He was going to prove his love to Brielle, even if the entire town of Sterling thought him nothing but a lovesick idiot.

That's what he was, wasn't he?

"You know you're going to set her house on fire, don't you?"

Colt turned to find Hawk walking toward him. "Not now, Hawk. She should be here any minute," Colt said, turning to pace the length of her porch yet again.

"When I got calls from three of her ranch hands who were concerned that you aren't in your right mind, I figured I had best come out to investigate," Hawk said as he came up onto the porch and then kept in step with Colt.

"The candles are all in jars," Colt pointed out before stopping and looking around, making sure the scene was still set.

Her entire front railing was covered in lighted candles. There were three hundred of them. He knew this for sure, because he'd lit every single one himself.

"You do know that with the dry weather, if even one of these jars tips over, the place could go up in flames, right?"

Of course Hawk had to say it — he was the fire chief. But it was also Colt's prerogative to ignore him. "If it burns, I'll build her a better house," Colt said before he resumed pacing, not even thinking about what an arrogant statement he'd just made.

"All right. Since Tony has the fire tender on standby, I guess I'll let you be." Hawk patted Colt on the shoulder and stepped down from the porch to go and sit with Tony, who, sure enough, had the fire truck backed up to the house. He was in a chair behind it, hose in his hand in case he needed to act quickly.

"It would sure help if you'd just go away, Tony," Colt snapped for what seemed like the tenth time.

"Not gonna happen, Colt," Tony drawled.

This was not going according to plan, Colt thought with frustration. Then everything else disappeared, because he saw headlights in the distance. That had to be Brielle — unless the hands had called in the sheriff, too.

Colt wouldn't have put that past them. Still, with his heart thundering and the blood rushing through his veins, he had no doubt it was Brielle. He could feel it. His mood lifted, his heart raced, and a smile returned to his face.

He planned to spend the rest of his life proving to this woman each and every day how much he loved her, and to treat her like the princess he knew she was.

But first he had to convince her to allow him in her life. Much easier said than done…

CHAPTER THIRTY-SIX

EXHAUSTION SEEMED TO be her middle name now, but Brielle was happy to be driving down the long road that led to her home. And yes, this was her home. She'd enjoyed the visit with her oldest brother, loved meeting his soon-to-be fiancée — at least if Crew had anything to say about it — and loved spending time with her father and getting to know her uncles, but she was glad to be home.

What a different drive this was for her now. The first time she'd taken this road, she'd been ticked off, miserable, and certain that her life was over. And it was — life as she'd once known it was over. But that was a good thing.

Unfortunately, Colt lived nearby. Talk about ambivalence.

Her anger was long gone, but that didn't mean she could just forget what he'd done. If only her foolish heart agreed with her mind. But the longer she was away from him, the more she yearned for his touch.

No. Impossible. How would she ever know for sure that he wanted her and not her land? Was it still about the land? She hadn't lied to him. She had to remember that and harden her heart to him.

When she turned the corner, she noticed a strange glow coming from her house. "What the…?" she said aloud.

When she pulled up, she realized her porch was lit up with…candles. Yes, those were candles, what appeared to be hundreds and hundreds of candles on her railing. As she emerged from the truck, she found Colt standing on her front deck, his arms at his sides, his whole body tense.

To her left, she saw Tony and Hawk sitting in a couple of lawn chairs beside the ranch's fire truck, but she barely glanced their way. Her eyes were drawn to one place — to the man now coming down the front steps.

They met halfway and she stood before him. But she didn't know what to say. *Just leave*?

"I've missed you, Brielle." His softly spoken words were nearly her undoing. But somehow she did manage to find her voice.

"What are you doing, Colt?"

"I can't go another day without seeing you, Brielle. When I close my eyes, I'm holding you."

"Colt, please just give it up."

"I can't. Though I know it's only a dream, it feels so real. I picture myself running my fingers through your long red hair, I feel the tremor in your body when we touch. Feelings like I've never felt before rush through me, and then I find myself with my lips brushing against yours. I imagine that hitch in your breathing, that small indication that you're as moved as I am each and every time we touch. Then I open my eyes and you aren't there. Everything disappears and I'm left with only emptiness. I want to close my eyes again, live in that perfect moment of having you in my arms."

"Colt…"

She was close to tears, and she didn't know what to say. He was offering his soul with so much passion, so much love. It had to be real. There was no way it couldn't be.

"Did you know that every time I come near you, I'm afraid of the way you affect me? And afraid of the way I need you. Or I *was* afraid. I thought I was happy before I met you, Brielle. I wasn't. And when I look into your eyes, I feel like I've found what my life has always been missing. And I didn't know there was something missing until recently, but now that I've had you by my side, I can never go back to the existence I walked through before you, to the way I was. You make me feel like I'm flying. You are worth holding onto forever, and I won't throw this away. I promise that if you give me another chance, I will never again treat you with disrespect, and I will never tell another untruth. I will hold you, care for you, and *love* you."

Brielle didn't try to stop the tears anymore. This man did love her — her! — spoiled little Brielle Storm who'd needed her father's intervention to help her find herself. Somehow, Colt had managed to see past her facade. And he actually liked the woman hiding inside. When he dropped to his knees in front of her and pulled out a black velvet jeweler's box, her knees shook.

"Brielle, please end my misery. Please be my wife — help make me a better man."

His eyes shone bright in the light from the candles behind them and the full moon filling the starry sky, and Brielle couldn't stand up a second longer. Sinking to her knees in front of him, she placed her hands on his face and brushed her lips against his.

"I don't want to live another day without you either, Colt," she whispered, and she wrapped her arms around his neck.

"I love you, Brielle." He ran his hands up and down her back, pushing the last of her worries away.

"I love you, too, Colt. Yes, I'll marry you. My heart won't let me do anything else."

He sat back, and she felt bereft until he lifted her hand, pulled out a flawless square-cut diamond, and slipped the ring on her finger — a perfect fit.

"You are my everything," he told her, and he sealed their promise to each other with a kiss.

Tony and Hawk had to turn away from the stirring scene, and from each other. The two gruff men were too touched by the beautiful moment they'd just witnessed.

After Colt carried Brielle through the front door, the two men outside put out all the candles, and then the only light shining down on the old ranch house was from the stars, which seemed to be twinkling a little more brightly on one of the last nights of summer.

EPILOGUE

"It looks as if we'll be getting at least two weddings this year," Richard said as he enjoyed a nice scotch with his brothers.

"Yes. I truly admire Colt," Joseph said. "Always have."

"Well, of course you do, because he's a good man. I'm just grateful I found that land. My only complaint is I missed most of the romance."

"You were pretty lucky in that match," George said with a laugh.

"I knew Brielle would end up on the ranch, and the first time I met Colt, he was an ornery cuss, but I liked and respected him. I had hoped sparks would fly, but hadn't held out much hope for it," Richard said. "I knew when I told the kids what I wanted from them that they would all be mad, but I also knew that Brielle would take the longest to accept her challenge, and there was just no way any of the boys would want anything to do with ranching. It seems each of the businesses I purchased has landed in the right hands, at least so far."

"Are you ever going to tell her you were hoping she and Colt would find each other?" George asked.

"Are you insane? She'd skin me alive."

"Yeah, that's pretty much how our kids feel," Joseph said. "But that doesn't matter. All that matters is the end result, and that's a lot of grandbabies and great-nieces and -nephews. I only wish we'd known each other when this 'journey' you've placed your children on started. There's nothing I like more than a bit of meddling."

"I couldn't agree with you more, brother," Richard said. "Plus, I'm way behind in the grandchild department, so it will be a pleasure catching up with you."

"From the way Colt and Brielle were looking at each other on our last visit, I bet it won't take long at all," Joseph told him.

"I think it's time to visit with Lance again. I want to see what that boy is up to. I have a feeling he's going to be my favorite nephew," George said with a smile.

"Ah, they're all my favorites," Joseph said, and he meant it. There wasn't one of the kids he loved more than the other. Okay, he did have to admit that his granddaughter Jasmine had an extra-special place in his heart.

"Even the strongest of them fall, George. Lance will fight to the end, but it's only a matter of time before he gives in to his destiny, and that certainly includes true love..." Richard said.

The three men clinked glasses.

Continue reading for an excerpt from the third book in *The Lost Andersons:*

Holiday
Treasure
Book Three in The Lost Andersons

PROLOGUE

TANNER STORM LEANED back comfortably in his chair as his sister, Brielle, vented her wrath and her frustration.

"How are you so damn calm, Tanner?" she shouted as she paced back and forth in the front room of his plush penthouse. "The old man has ripped everything from us! Everything!"

"He can't take what he doesn't know about," Tanner said, not fazed the least.

"What are you talking about? He froze all of my assets, my cards, everything. He stopped my payments on bills. I will be homeless soon and he doesn't even care. If I don't play his stupid little game, then I am screwed."

What neither his father nor his siblings knew was that Tanner had his own wealth. He hadn't been close to his family in a very long time, and he hadn't wasted all his time away. He'd taken a different path than any of them, and he'd managed to make some incredibly good investments. But he didn't want any of them to know.

Yes, he could help his sister out, but for some odd reason, he wasn't positive that he wanted to. Sure, their dad's little lesson — to teach them all how to be responsible — was pretty laughable, and Tanner knew it, but unless he wanted his family to find out everything, what could he do but play along when the old man decided to put on his puppet show?

When he'd been landed with this sorry building as a test to see whether he was worthy to be reinstated as an heir to the old guy's empire, he'd thought it nothing but a joke — a very annoying joke, but a joke nonetheless, with no laughs anywhere in sight. But no, it was right there in black and white on his father's letterhead.

One part of Tanner wanted to play the game, wanted to take one of his father's projects and make it succeed. It would prove to the old man that his son was not someone to write off so easily. Another part of him wanted to tell his father to stick it where the sun didn't shine.

Ah, he still hadn't made up his mind. How was he to follow his dad's terms and make a go of the stupid place? But when he'd checked out the property, he couldn't help but grow excited. Even now, brick and mortar could make a rational man see dollar signs.

Looking at his sister, a woman of beauty and intelligence, and someone he'd once thought the sun rose and fell upon, made him even more determined to prove their father wrong. Somewhere along the way, his family had fallen apart.

Was his father doing a good thing? No. Tanner wouldn't take it that far. But still…

He tuned back in, and his sister's ranting helped Tanner make his decision. He would accept his father's project, dammit. He would take the failing apartment complex his father had bought and he would rip it down and put in its place something so beautiful, so amazing, so profitable, that his father would have to admit he'd been wrong about his son.

Tanner suddenly wanted to get started. This project was stirring his blood, exciting him. It would be a lot of fun, and fun wasn't something he'd had in a long time.

"Brielle," he said with sudden determination, "you can pace and cry all you want, but the bottom line is that you either accept this or not. We might not always like what's thrown our way, but our character is defined by the decisions we make." He stood up and moved toward the door with a gesture whose meaning was clear — *follow me and get out.*

He was fed up with his sister's tantrum, and he really didn't want to deal with her any longer.

"You're a jerk, Tanner. You always have been and always will be," she said, grabbing her purse and following him.

"Sorry, sweetheart, but I just don't…care."

His smile, if you could call it that, made his sister glare at him before she walked out his door.

As he shut it, the smile fell away. Yes, he *was* a jerk, someone who pushed anyone and everyone away from him. But wasn't that the way he wanted to be? It sure as hell made his life more comfortable and efficient. Yes, he was managing quite well, he told himself as he went toward his study.

He had a project to head, and he wasn't going to waste any more time. Once Tanner Storm set his mind to something, he didn't stop until it was finished.

CHAPTER ONE

"MR. STORM, YOU ay think that you're above the law, but I guarantee you that you are not! This is the fourth time I've seen you in my courtroom in the last three months. It's become a bad habit, one that I don't appreciate. I don't care how much you're paying your group of attorneys. It's not getting you out of trouble this time."

"Your Honor—"

The judge did not take kindly to Tanner Storm's interruption. "Do not make me add contempt of court to your list of crimes," Judge Kragle said. "The conditions of your building are deplorable. I'm absolutely appalled that you'd leave women and children with no working elevators, with corroding pipes, and *with no heat*. I've thought long and hard about your punishment—"

"Your Honor," Tanner's attorney broke in, "Mr. Storm has been trying to get the building condemned since he took ownership six months ago. If the tenants would take his incredibly generous offer to vacate, they could relocate to a much safer environment for their families, and he could tear the building down and start the project he has made plans for already."

"Mr. Henry, sit down," the judge said. "I've read through the files — I'm not blind. Mr. Storm has made it more than clear that he looks down his nose at this building, which he seemed to receive as a consolation prize in some family game of inheritances and trust funds. Don't insult my intelligence by telling me that Mr. Storm has these people's best interests at heart. The complex that he plans to build wouldn't be even *marginally* affordable to the current tenants, who are struggling to make ends meet *without* having the added pressure of moving." Judge Kragle's voice was quiet but stern, especially when he wanted to emphasize any of his remarks.

Tanner's first attorney obediently sat down, but another one rose in his place.

"You may not like our client, Your Honor, but he's well within his legal rights," said this attorney, a well-known shark, his demeanor confident, his suit costing more than most people paid for a car.

"No, Mr. Silt, he most certainly is *not* obeying the law. If you've managed to forget, the jury has already rendered its verdict, and not in your client's favor. We are now in the *sentencing* phase — remember that? — *and* I've made my decision. Tanner Storm, please rise," the judge said, a smile of pure satisfaction on his face that made Tanner more than a bit nervous, and nerves weren't usually part of his psychic makeup. "It seems that you haven't learned from your previous experiences standing before me, so I've decided to try a different penalty. You'll spend three days in jail, beginning immediately after I've finished here."

There was a murmur in the courtroom, everyone shocked that Judge Kragle would dare send Tanner Storm, the son of a billionaire, to jail. Tanner just smiled. He'd be out in six hours, max. He had nothing to worry about.

"After your jail sentence, you'll be under house arrest in the same building your tenants are living in. You will live there for twenty-four days, starting the first day of December, and ending on Christmas Day, December Twenty-Fifth."

The judge paused, and Tanner's eyes widened in shock. He felt his first stirrings of real unease. There was no way that he could stay in that building for such an extended time. It didn't even have Internet access. How was he supposed to get anything done?

"Furthermore, you aren't allowed to do any updates, additions, construction, repairs, or alterations on your own apartment that you don't provide for the rest of the building first," the judge continued. "If you want to bring the comforts of home to the complex, be my guest, but *your* unit will be the last to be worked on. The conditions of the building are appalling, and it would do you some good to learn a bit of humility. Your father is a good man, a man who is obviously trying to teach you much-needed respect for those around you. He has served this community well since moving here, and he has given you this opportunity in the hopes that you will do the right thing."

"But—" Tanner was getting desperate.

"I'm not finished! You will also be required to serve one hundred and twenty hours of community service during your time."

"I can't serve all those hours and still do my job," Tanner burst out, fury overcoming his usual discretion.

"I guess you'll have to take time off from work, Mr. Storm. You will serve every single hour or I'll impose the full sentence allowed by law — five years in a state prison."

Judge Kragle sat back and looked Tanner in the eye. Tanner attempted to exude confidence, but the set of his incredibly high-priced attorneys' shoulders told him more than anything that he just wasn't getting out of this.

"Do I need to scrub some graffiti off ghetto walls?" Tanner made no attempt to hide his sarcasm. He had donated astronomical amounts of money to charity in his life; his time, however, was priceless, and he wasn't happy about having to share it — to waste it, probably.

"No, Mr. Storm. You'll be volunteering as Santa Claus this season."

When the judge banged his gavel, Tanner stared back in horror as the courtroom erupted. Reporters tried in vain to get a statement from him as — the grossest indignity of all — he was handcuffed and led away through a back door.

Merry freaking Christmas to him!

CHAPTER TWO

TANNER GROUND HIS teeth while he packed a bag. Nope. Wouldn't need his hand-tailored suits. Nope. Wouldn't need his Rolex. Nope. Wouldn't need anything he had in his penthouse on top of a luxury high-rise in downtown Seattle.

Anything he took with him to his temporary prison would stay behind when he left. He wouldn't want to bring back the filth he was sure was going to seep into his very bones while he stayed in that wretched building for three long weeks and change.

He'd fought the judge's orders — paid a lot of his own money to his useless attorneys to get him out of this ridiculous sentence. They'd been sweating as they told him they couldn't get the judge's ruling overturned. Tanner delivered a savage kick to his newly bought duffel bag, which had the misfortune to be lying in his path.

"Are you almost ready, Mr. Storm?"

Tanner nearly growled at the two officers waiting in his doorway. He hadn't even been allowed to come back to his penthouse without escorts. No. They thought he might be a flight risk. Damn right he was a flight risk.

They'd slapped some ridiculous contraption on his ankle as if he were a real criminal, and they were hauling him by police car to the apartment building in what had been one of the less affluent parts of the city.

Still, over the past decade, the city *had* vastly improved the area near where the building was located, and the site was ideal for a profitable project. With Tanner designing and building, the area would be brand new and his bank account would grow even fatter.

But nothing had gone right since he'd taken over the damned place. He'd been trying to buy off the tenants, get them to leave, and get going on demolition, but only half the people had taken his more than generous offer. The remaining tenants flatly refused to budge.

His legal team hadn't found any loopholes yet, so he'd left it to his very efficient business crew to help out. He hadn't *known* the heat in the building had been turned off — and then crapped out completely — and if he'd been aware of his employees' plans, he would have called an immediate halt. He wasn't a monster. Not that the judge had let him get that far in his explanations.

"Not yet," Tanner finally snapped at the officers. Their impatience was becoming almost palpable as he took his sweet time.

Tanner was beginning to think that proving his father wrong just wasn't worth it. But he'd already started down this path and he certainly wouldn't be called a quitter. No, he'd pretend to be a party his father's scheme for family reunification — for now. But only because he saw the potential it had to add to his own portfolio. He'd construct a new complex in place of the monstrosity his father had given him. Piece of cake, piece of lucrative cake. He just had to get the stupid tenants to vacate first.

Because his father had put certain annoying clauses in the contract, Tanner couldn't force the people out; all he could do was offer them generous moving packages. Why did everything have to be so difficult? He should tell his father to kiss off and just walk away from the whole project. And it would have been so easy to do that. Why did the though turn his stomach?

Okay, okay. He loved his family, even if they'd run into a few speed bumps over the years.

Crew was now married and in love, happier than Tanner had ever seen him. Well, that was good for his brother, but none of that was in the cards for him. He was just trying to make an honest buck — well, an honest billion bucks — and between his father and this freaking Judge Kragle, he was hitting walls left and right.

Tanner searched for the running shoes his assistant had picked up for him. He'd sent the man out to buy all new clothes from a local mall.

When Tanner was down at those decaying apartments, he didn't want to be tabloid fodder.

Hell, he didn't know how to shop, hadn't done it, well, ever that he could remember. Yes, he'd shopped with short-term girlfriends in some high-end malls on the banks of the Seine, but he'd never once entered a middle-class mall, or any mall, in America.

Wearing the scratchy jail clothes for the last three days had been seriously unpleasant, and he was determined to ban the color orange from his sight. But how much better were things now? For three weeks, or more accurately, twenty-four painful days, he was going to be stuck in denim and cotton, and even worse.

Polyester.

Tomorrow he had to put on a flipping Santa costume. Just the thought made his head itch. Who knew how many sweaty bodies had been in the same suit? He'd insisted that his assistant have it professionally cleaned. At least the senile judge had allowed him that much.

The man obviously needed to retire. It was long overdue and the judge looked like freaking Santa Claus himself. Maybe Judge Kragle should be the one down at the mall letting a bunch of sticky, snot-nosed brats climb all over *him*.

"Let's go," one of the officers said, this time not as pleasantly.

Tanner had dragged his feet long enough. If he didn't walk with them willingly, the fuzz were going to throw the handcuffs back on him and escort him through the building in a far less dignified manner than by simply walking behind him.

This day just kept on getting better.

He'd at least managed to talk the officers into allowing him to leave through his private penthouse entrance. The last thing he wanted at his exclusive high-rise was for anyone, rich, poor, or in between, to see him being escorted off to the cheap streets by some of Seattle's finest.

Undignified? As if!

Stepping from his apartment, he gave a long-suffering sigh as he pushed the elevator button and moved inside.

"Don't you guys have more important things to do than escort a law-abiding citizen around?" Tanner asked.

One of the officers threw his a scornful glance. "Are you suggesting that we're slackers, *Mister* Tanner?"

"I would never think that," Tanner replied. "I was just saying that there are people out there who are *actually* committing crimes, and yet you're both here 'escorting' me when I've never broken the law in my life."

"I beg to differ, Mr. Storm," the other officer snapped. "My *mother* lives in your *new* apartment complex. Or the *older* of the two that you happen to have. I think that having you stay there is sweet justice. Maybe this Christmas you'll actually find a heart." The guy snickered despite himself.

"Didn't your mother tell you that I offered each tenant a large sum to move out?"

"I hate men like you, men who think they can solve all the world's problems by throwing their wallets around. My mom has been in that building for thirty-five years. She has friends there, history, and she doesn't want to leave. She just wants the heat and water to work correctly, and for rodents and bugs to not crawl all over everything she owns."

"That's the exact reason I want to condemn the building and start over," Tanner said. He couldn't hide his frustration.

"The building is solid, and it wouldn't take much to bring it up to code," the officer told him heatedly. "You just need to get your priorities straight."

Tanner didn't feel like saying anything else as the elevator doors opened and the three of them stepped out into the garage.

The police car was waiting for him. When he hit his head as they *helped* him inside, his lips compressed.

Twenty-four days. He just had to remember this would be for only twenty-four days.

CHAPTER THREE

AS TANNER FOUND himself traveling the streets of Seattle in the back of a smelly police cruiser, he decided he was done talking to anyone and everyone. When they arrived at what would be his home for more than the next three miserable weeks, he couldn't keep the disgusted look from his face as one the officers opened the back door and grinned — yes, it was the one whose mother lived in the building. Tanner didn't feel too protected right now, and he really wanted to point out to both officers that it was their job to *serve and protect*, wasn't it?

But this cop was enjoying the authority part of his job far too much for Tanner's liking — the guy looked as if he was itching to use his club, or even his gun. He was probably another underpaid public servant who thought men like Tanner needed to be knocked down a peg or two. No respect for the people who ensured he had a job by paying so much in taxes. Or it seemed like a lot, anyway.

"Have a pleasant stay, Mr. Storm," the officer said before tipping his hat and leaving Tanner standing on the broken sidewalk.

Those cops weren't worried he'd run now. They'd find him instantly, because of the device on his damned ankle. Thank the heavens the thing wasn't too big and he could hide it with a thick pair of socks. His humiliation would be complete if anyone saw the depths to which he'd fallen.

Deciding his self-pity party had gone on long enough, Tanner pulled hard on the building's heavy front door, which desperately needed some lubricant on the hinges. He was grateful to see no one about as he began his trek down the hallway. He wasn't there to make friends, and he didn't feel like speaking to a single person. The only people he'd likely find living here willingly were the type for whom burning in hell seemed appropriate.

Tanner reached his apartment, and he was almost afraid to open the door. The hallways weren't cluttered, but the paint was peeling and there was a musty smell in the air that suggested leaks no one had bothered to patch up. He was sure mold was running rampant throughout the place.

That had to be a health risk — wouldn't it allow him to have the building condemned? He hadn't even bothered looking through the reports from the inspection yet — he left that kind of thing to his employees. Maybe it was time he went through them himself, line by line. He did have a lot of extra time on his hands for most of the next month, even with all the hours he had to spend wearing a Santa costume. All he knew for sure was that he wanted to tear the outdated building down and start fresh. It would certainly be a lot less hassle.

His legal team had quickly put the kibosh on the crap about historical value that local societies had spouted. Anyway, he couldn't care less if the crown moldings had been handcrafted by early settlers of the area.

He wanted new. He wanted modern.

Squaring his shoulders, Tanner stepped inside his "new" apartment and looked around. The size of the place surprised him. A large living room was separated by a breakfast bar from a decent-sized kitchen. The appliances were extremely outdated, but the apartment wasn't as filthy as he was expecting.

Huge windows opened out onto the grungy street, but Tanner saw potential for the neighborhood, especially since every area except the one with his building had been cleaned up. The riffraff living here ensured that this particular neighborhood remained sketchy, but he'd been told that respectable businesses would come back if this building was replaced. Nearby, a new complex was in line to be completed next year. Things were improving, dammit.

But he had to think about the here and now. And it could be worse. Down a short hallway, he found a roomy bathroom, again with outdated fixtures, but still decently clean. Then there were two bedrooms — with ridiculously small closets. Okay, maybe they weren't that small, but he was used to having everything fit for a darn king. That thought brought his first smile of the day. It quickly disappeared when he heard someone call out.

"Hello?"

Who in the world would be coming into his place uninvited? No one even knew he was here, not even his brothers and his sister. He hadn't wanted to tell anyone. If his siblings got word that he was being forced to don a Santa suit, they'd be first in line to point cameras directly at him.

His only consolation was that the judge hadn't listed where he was to do his community service when the reporters swarmed around him after the hearing was over. He didn't doubt that they'd figure it out, though. This would be too juicy a photo op for anyone in the media to pass up. He'd just keep his fingers crossed that it didn't happen.

Walking back out to the living room, he found a petite blonde with bright blue eyes looking at him, a welcoming smile on her face. Before he was able to say anything, she spoke.

"Your door was open, so I thought I'd see who was in here. They've frozen any of the apartments from being rented, so..." Her meaning was loud and clear. She thought he was a vagrant who had found a warm place to sleep.

Jeez. She wasn't the brightest bulb on the Christmas tree to be confronting someone who could be a criminal.

He approached her. "I won't be here long," he replied, his manner stiff. "But I am living here for now. Do you always just walk into other people's homes?"

His unpleasant tone made her take a step back, and he had to give her a few points for at least being a bit nervous.

"Sorry about that, but like I said, your door was open and these apartments aren't being rented," she said, leaving it hanging in the air. When he said nothing, she went on. "How long are you staying?" She didn't look him in the eye this time, but instead looked around the empty room. Nothing in it except for one large duffel bag.

"That's undetermined right now," he told her. He'd learned never to give out too much information and he didn't care at all what this woman thought about him, so he decided to let her wonder how he'd managed to rent an unrentable apartment.

The woman looked at him with wide eyes and a wavering smile, but she still just stood there, as if trying to determine whether she could trust him or not. What if he were a serial killer? Did she have no self-preservation instincts at all?

"I've lived here for two years. It's a great place if you can get past the mice," she said with a laugh. "At least there are a lot of storage areas."

"Mice?" Tanner looked around uneasily.

"Yeah, but I've named them, so I'm not so scared of the little critters anymore."

"Named them?" Tanner almost found it amusing that he kept repeating what she said. Almost.

"Yeah, you know, like in *Cinderella*. Or *A Little Princess* — but Melchisidec was a rat, and there's a difference, of course. I would say the Disney mice would help you unpack, but you don't really have anything here. Were you making sure you liked the place first?"

Tanner realized that he hadn't ordered a bed, a couch, anything. He wasn't looking forward to being here, and he just hadn't thought that far ahead. Of course he would need some basics, even for only from now until Christmas. His assistant should have been on top of this. Maybe it was time to hire a new one.

"Everything will be delivered later today," Tanner said as he moved toward the door. Would this woman take the hint?

"Oh, not having to move it yourself must be nice. I despise moving. It's so physically and emotionally exhausting and then you *always* lose something in the process — every single time, no matter how organized you are or how carefully you label the boxes."

"Yes, moving is unpleasant," Tanner said dryly. "Well, I have some phone calls to make…" He held open the door she'd blown past when entering his place *illegally*. He'd really begun to care about legality.

"I'm sorry. I'll leave you be. My name is Kyla, by the way, Kyla Ridgley." She walked right up to him and held out her hand.

Tanner looked at it for a moment as if he didn't know what to do, but then his manners kicked in and he held out his own hand. "Tanner," he offered, and nothing more.

"Well, it's great to meet you, Tanner," she said, and then her warm, slender hand was somehow clasped in his.

Tanner nearly took a step back when their fingers touched. It felt like a spark had just ignited between the two of them.

"Um, as I said, great to meet you," Kyla almost gasped. She jerked her hand from his and dashed through his door.

When she slipped inside the apartment right across the hall from his and quickly closed the door behind her, Tanner stared for several moments at the space she'd been occupying.

Maybe his "jail" time had just become a lot more bearable. With a slight smile lifting the corners of his mouth, he picked up his phone to call his assistant.

Furniture was his first priority.

Then, he was going to find out a bit more about his new neighbor. A three-week fling might just make this situation a whole lot easier to swallow.

Made in the USA
San Bernardino, CA
11 December 2015